Herodotus, Andrew Lang, Barnabe Rich

Euterpe

being the second book of the famous History of Herodotus

Herodotus, Andrew Lang, Barnabe Rich

Euterpe
being the second book of the famous History of Herodotus

ISBN/EAN: 9783337191771

Printed in Europe, USA, Canada, Australia, Japan

Cover: Foto ©Andreas Hilbeck / pixelio.de

More available books at **www.hansebooks.com**

Euterpe : Being the Second Book of the

Famous History of Herodotus.

Englished by B. R. 1584.

Edited by Andrew

Lang.

LONDON. M.D.CCCLXXXVIII. PUBLISHED BY DAVID
NUTT, IN THE STRAND.

TO

COLONEL HENRY YULE.

Herodotus in Egypt.

HE left the land of youth, he left the young,
  The smiling Gods of Greece, he passed the isle
Where Jason loitered, and where Sappho sung :
  He sought the secret-founted wave of Nile,
  Of that old world, half dead a weary while ;
Heard the Priests murmur in their mystic tongue,
  And through the fanes went voyaging, among
Dark tribes that worshipped Cat and Crocodile.

He learned the tales of death Divine and birth,
Strange loves of hawk and serpent, Sky and Earth,
  The marriage and the slaying of the Sun ;
The shrines of ghosts and beasts he wandered through,
And mocked not at their godhead, for he knew
  Behind all creeds the Spirit that is One.—A. L.

To Herodotus.

FAR-TRAVELLED coaster of the Midland seas !
What marvels did those curious eyes behold,—
Winged snakes, and carven labyrinths of old ;
The emerald column raised to Heracles,
King Perseus' shrine upon the Chemmian leas,
Four-footed fishes, decked with gems and gold :
But thou didst leave some secrets yet untold,
And veiled the dread Osirian mysteries.

And now the golden asphodels among
Thy footsteps fare, and to the lordly dead
Thou tellest all the stories left unsaid
Of secret rites and runes forgotten long,
Of that dark folk who ate the Lotus-bread,
And sang the melancholy Linus-song.

—G. R. T.

PREFACE.

This translation of the second book of Herodotus, the book on Egypt, is reprinted from a
sufficiently rare volume, "*THE* | Famous Hys-
tory of | *HERODOTUS* | *Conteyning the Dis-
course* of dyuers Countreys, the succession | *of
theyr Kyngs: the actes and exploytes* | atchieuved
by them, the Lawes and | customes of every
Nation : with the | true Description and Anti-
quitie of the same. | Deuided into nine Bookes,
entituled with | the names of the nine Muses. |
AT LONDON. | Printed by Thomas Marshe.
1584." |

The little quarto only contains Books i. and ii.
The Dedication runs :—" To the right excellent
and virtuous *Gentleman Mayster Robert Dormer*,
sonne to the noble Knight Sir Wyllyam Dormer,
B. R. wisheth increase of worship, with the
favoure of God." Who is B. R. ? Barnaby
Rich has been guessed at ; nothing is certainly
known. He writes in a very colloquial style,
too colloquial for Herodotus, and his pages are

a treasure of old English slang. He is as inaccurate, or as careless of close rendering rather, as may be. But B. R. tells a story with point, with breadth; above all, with enjoyment. Of what other translator of Herodotus can we say as much! Not of Beloe the proverbially flat, nor of Rawlinson the respectable.

As to the book itself, it is not common. Besides that in the British Museum, I have only seen a copy once belonging to Mr. Payne Collier, and now to the Rev. W. J. Loftie, and my own copy, which, I am happy to say, is much taller, cleaner, and in better case than Mr. Loftie's. The Editor may end by hoping that a new translator of Herodotus will arise, as lively as B. R.; less addicted to slang, and as accurate as modern scholarship can make him.

THE
RELIGION OF HERODOTUS.

HERODOTUS in Egypt is one of the most curious and attractive figures in the most singular group of people and circumstances. He comes as the envoy of a race with a strong sense of its own youth, to a race already conscious of antiquity and of decay. A considerable expanse of time, which he regarded as historic (1000 years, see ii. 145), lay behind Herodotus in Hellas. He thinks Homer some four hundred years his senior, and behind Homer he discerns other

figures of elder poets and priests, warriors and
soothsayers, Orpheus, Danaus, Melampus. Yet
he feels that even the remotest persons in the
legends of his race are of yesterday, compared
with the dark backward of Egypt. Curious on
all questions of origins, Herodotus first (for of
Hecatæus we have received little) brings Egypt
under the light of European inquiry. Acknow-
ledging the great age of civilisation in the valley
of the Nile, he looks there for the beginnings
of knowledge—knowledge about men and gods,
beasts and omens, arts and manufactures. The
tendency to believe that institutions, myths,
customs, were not developed alike under many
skies, but were invented in one place, and were
thence carried about the world, was powerful in
the thought of Herodotus. It is a tendency still
very vivacious, and the learned frequently endea-
vour to account for a myth or rite in a country
new to them by supposing that it was brought
from a country to them familiar, generally from
India or Babylon, according to taste. Herodotus,
in the course of his inquiry into all human and
divine things, naturally adopts this line of conjecture. Wherever he discovers a resemblance
between a Greek god or a Greek sacrifice or

mystery, and an Egyptian sacrifice, mystery, or
god, he is apt to conclude that the thing or the
deity was brought from Egypt. He was well
aware that Greece had dealings with the land of
Khem even in times before history : Homer bore
witness to this, and Cyrus spoke of Egyptian
settlers in Argos and of Io, who wandered, gad-
driven, from Argos back to Egypt. Herodotus thus
relied on a *vera causa.* There had been actual
intercourse between heroic Greece and Egypt. If
similar institutions were found in the two lands,
it was natural to conclude that the younger had
borrowed from the elder—borrowed gods and
ways of worshipping them. Herodotus could
hardly be expected to suggest that similar work-
ings of similar minds in similar circumstances
might have produced similarities of thought,
practice, and belief. With his firm conviction
that young Greece was but old Egypt's pupil,
he came to the mystic Osirian land, expecting,
perhaps, to discover something old, yet something true, about the nature of the gods and
their relations to men. The questions, the eternal
questions, had been mooted by Xenophanes and
Empedocles. Were the gods the capricious folk
of myths ? Were they of human speech and

shape? Were they bond-slaves of necessity? Were
they jealous or kindly? In Egypt Herodotus
might hope to hear some whisper of ancient
wisdom, to lift for a moment the star-sown veil
of Isis.

Herodotus, in his Theology, is chiefly moved,
like the author of the Book of Job, by the spec-
tacle of the changes and chances in the world.
Do the gods rule the destinies of men? Do they
reward and punish human conduct? Are the
vast vicissitudes of empires, the fall and rise of
men, due to the divine justice or the divine
jealousy? Can the ways of God or of gods be
justified to men? This is, in truth, the gist of
the Histories of Herodotus. With all his many
curiosities about every trait of manners, every
turn of events, every variation of morals in different conditions, what he is most curious about
is the nature of the Divine, and of its human
relations. The whirling wheel of fortune (i. 207)
he contemplates as it is contemplated by the
Buddha—from without. " Who moves it? Why
does it abase the mighty and raise the weak?"
he asks. " Τὴν ἀνθρωπηίην ὦν ἐπιστάμενος εὐδαιμονίην
οὐδαμὰ ἐν τὠυτῷ μένουσαν, ἐπιμνήσομαι ἀμφοτέρων
ὁμοίως;" (i. 5).

" How low men are, and how they rise,
How high they were, and how they tumble ;
O vanity of vanities,
O laughable pathetic jumble !"

Is it mere vanity, the Greek traveller asks, or
is there something to be known of the hand
behind the curtain that moves the kings and
pawns on the board? Concerning all this there
was no certainty in the home of eloquence and
music, in the isles of song. It might be that
"the meanest of the sacristans of Isis knew
more than they." On the whole, Herodotus is
disposed to believe in somewhat that is neither
quite impersonal fate, nor quite a personal God,
or gods—in τὸ θεῖον. "The Divine," says Solon,
"is ever jealous, and delights to disturb the
affairs of men" (i. 32). This is but a half philosophical statement of the popular belief in the
evil eye, of the instinctive dread which makes
the Cyclopes, in Theocritus, spit in his breast
when he deems himself beautiful (vi. 39). This
superstition has a rational basis, like others.
Pride goes before a fall, because pride walks
proudly, not looking to its steps. But the popular fancy has always conceived some vague force
to which pride and prosperity are distasteful,

and to which Polycrates vainly sacrificed his Ring.

This is τὸ θεῖον in Herodotus; this, more than aught else, is the metaphysical and scientific basis of his religious beliefs. "God has shown a sight of happiness to many men, and then has overthrown them utterly" (i. 32, vii. 105). "Great wrath (Nemesis) from God fell on Crœsus, belike because he deemed himself of all men the most fortunate" (i. 34). Here "God" and "the Divine" are equivalents for each other: there is no polytheistic notion, unless by "the god" we are to understand Apollo, the deity best worshipped by Crœsus. It is immediately after telling the varied tale of Apollo's dealings with Crœsus, and of the Lydian's endeavours "to tempt God," that Herodotus mocks at earlier Athenian credulity. The device of Pisistratus, whereby the tall and fair Phya, in Athene's armour, brought him back to Athens like a goddess visible, seems to Herodotus "the most ridiculous contrivance" (i. 60). He declares that the Athenians, with all their boasted wit, worshipped the woman, and accepted the return of the tyrant. Clearly Herodotus regards the visible apparition of a god or goddess to a multi-

tude as no longer credible; yet, in other moods,
he can tell of Pan's message to the lonely way-
farer in the hills, and of the great ghostly
company that sped along the sacred way.

But his credulity again is overstrained by the
Æginetan fable, that the wooden statues of Damia
and Auxesia fell on their knees when the Athenians tried to drag them by ropes (v. 86). He
will not believe that gods lie with women in the
temples of Egyptian Thebes, or Babylon (i. 182).
On the other hand, the amazing legend of
Aristeas, who accompanied Apollo in the guise
of a crow, and who appeared in human form at
immense intervals of time, evokes no expression
of disbelief (iv. 15). Nor does Herodotus dis-
pute the beautiful miracle of Helen, who, in
Sparta, restored a deformed child to beauty; nor
does he cavil at the wrath of the dead Talthy-
bius (vi. 61, vii. 141). He is always ready to
be persuaded by oracles and dreams.

To give examples of these were superfluous.
Apparently he thinks that oracles are a kind
of vague light shown forth by the gods, or
by God, to guide or misguide men as their
own conduct and their own wisdom in in-
terpretation may chance to deserve. For the

b

Divine, to his mind, will not interfere too plainly, nor declare itself too manifestly, even within the region of the supernatural. Man must fight his own battle now with but vague and faint assistance. It is not as in Homer, where the gods appear manifestly, nor as of old in Phæacia. The divine tendency " makes for righteousness " and for the best. " The providence of God, as is natural, proves itself wise " (iii. 108). " There is a certain child of an oath," says the oracle, " which punishes the perjurer." The gods show forth signs and omens before the coming of a great disaster. They punish men who insult them directly by attacking their suppliants (v. 8). The gods are not ungrateful. When Crœsus fell, in spite of all his loyalty to Apollo, the oracle justified the ways of the god to the man, by announcing that " even the god cannot avoid the destined fate. Crœsus hath atoned for the crime of his ancestor in the fifth generation," namely, of Gyges, who slew his master. It would have been as easy to reply that Crœsus had carded an enemy to death with a fuller's thistle (i. 92), and that " the gods detest the excessive revenges of men " (iv. 205).

Such is the general Herodotean conception of

the divine government of the world. He holds a
kind of Theism, in which a spiritual conscious
force is limited in its action by destiny and by
circumstance, but never fails to punish human
arrogance. This is a theological way of con-
ceiving the precept Μηδὲν ἄγαν — the strong,
almost instinctive Greek sense of the beauty
and the necessity of Law and Limit. But in
this Herodotean divinity there is little of human
sweetness and charity. These qualities best
appear in the miracle wrought by Helen, and in
the "divine providence" which commanded the
child Cypselus to smile when in the hands of the
man who would have slain him—"And when the
man beheld it a certain pitifulness constrained
him not to slay the babe" (v. 92). But this
limited Divinity contrasts poorly with the rich
beauty of Greek mythology as it glows in Homer
and in art.

Herodotus pays little regard to questions as to
the separate aspects and characters of the gods.
It seems as if he had never felt disposed to
answer such questions in his own mind, or as if
his cautious reverence made him abstain. The
Divine, to his fancy, seems something undifferen-
tiated, to which local names and characters are

assigned by various races of men. Not that he would deny the separate existence of Osiris or of Dionysus. " A great ox hath trodden on his tongue," the bull Apis, and he is even provokingly silent about the mysteries and sacred stories that he has heard.

Could Herodotus have chosen a nation whose faith was to his mind, he would perhaps have selected the Persian (i. 131), at least if Persian custom corresponded to his theory of it. " It is not among their customs to raise statues, nor build temples, nor altars, and when others do so they reckon it against them as folly. To my thinking, because they do not hold that the gods have human form as do the Greeks. . . . The whole circle of Heaven they call Zeus. They sacrifice to sun and moon, to earth and stars, and water and wind." The worship of Mitra (Mylitta, or Alitta, or Ourania) they have learned from Arabians and Assyrians.[1]

As to the differentiating of the supernatural, the assignment to the mysterious force of different names, characters, and parts in the divine

---

[1] Professor Sayce (*Herodotos*, p. 78), says that Darius complains, at Behistun, that Gomates the Magian had destroyed "the temples of the gods."

comedy, Herodotus inclines, as has been said, to
find its origin in Egypt (ii. 50). What he means
by his assertion that the Greek names of deities
came thence (as the names in Greece and Egypt
are so totally different) it is hard to conjecture.
Professor Sayce offers no explanation, except that
Herodotus had "the same high opinion of the
Egyptians that many Englishmen have of the
French," and many more of the Germans. Perhaps Herodotus only meant that the *rôles* indicated by the names were originally Egyptian,
that the Egyptians assigned "departments" to
the gods, and that the Greeks followed their
example. He also finds known gods all the
world over: Dionysus and Urania as Orotal and
Alilat in Arabia (iii. 8); and in Scythia, Hestia,
Zeus, Apollo, Urania, Hercules, Ares, Poseidon.
These wear such names as Tabiti, Papæus, Apia,
Œtosyrus, Artimpasa, and Thauramasadas (iii.
59). Poseidon originally came from Libya. The
Greek gods that had no Egyptian counterparts
were, by origin, Pelasgian.

All this theory of borrowing is based by Herodotus on the close similarity of the rites of Osiris
and Dionysus (ii. 49). He could not believe that
the similarity came "by chance," and imagined

that Cadmus gave the ideas to Melampus. This argument would, of course, demonstrate that the rites of Aztecs and Zunis, when they resemble those of Egypt or Babylon, were carried to America from the Old World. The hypothesis of borrowing has always been a favourite with the learned. Now it is from Egypt, now from India, now from Phœnicia, now from Babylon that the myths and rituals of races are said to have set out. Canon Taylor has discovered that Psyche's is a Babylonian legend. It may be difficult, in many cases, to prove a negative, when intercommunication between races is possible.[1] But it is certain that the assignment of natural departments to gods, that Polytheism, in short, will always have an analogous character among races in certain stages of civilisation. Sahagun found many analogues of Greek gods in Mexico, but they were not borrowed from Greece nor from Babylon. If such ideas can be independently evolved, we may suspend the judgment when the learned ask us to believe that Greek myth and religion came from this or that alien centre, as fancy prompts or individual choice suggests.

[1] Gruppe, *Die Griech. Cult. und Myth.*, 150–171.

To Herodotus we owe the clearest foreign view
of Egyptian religion in his own time. The most
remarkable feature, doubtless, is the local animal worship. On this we have written so fully
(*Myth, Ritual, and Religion*, ii. 97–108) that it
would be tedious here to repeat all the argument.
On the whole, it appears probable to me that
Egyptian Religion, as far as we can trace it, is
woven of three strands of thought and belief.
The worship of the Dead, each of whom is an
Osiris, is one strand; the worship of great elemental forces and forms of things, Sun, Moon,
Heaven, Earth, is another strand; the worship,
in many localities, of a beast, bird, or fish not
sacred in another locality is a third strand.
The last I take to be, in many cases, a survival
of totemism. All these threads are antique, and
all are interwoven, over and under each other,
into a pattern of singular complexity. Osiris, at
first perhaps the name of the Home, and of the
King of the Dead, is identified with Sun, and
Stream, with each man's soul, with the soul of
all things. The same Osiris is bedizened, for
local reasons, in bestial heads, in fur and feather,
of ram and bull, crane and hawk. Political and
theological syncretism blends god with god,

symbols are mixed with symbols, myth with
myth, magic with theology : paternity and worship are diversely assigned. As Professor Sayce
says, "The animal forms of the gods take us
back to a remote prehistoric age, when the
religious creed of Egypt was still totemism"
(*Herodotos*, p. 344). But even totemists may
have had their stories of a divine Earth, and
Sun, and Heaven, and of Osiris, the King of the
country of the souls, the Mighty Warden of the
Ghosts. To illustrate one's theory and position
while enjoying a gentle wrangle dear to anti-
quarians, one may quote a learned reviewer of
my *Myth, Ritual, and Religion.* He says in the
St. James's Gazette (December 3, 1887) :—

"We may now proceed to examine the adequacy
of Mr. Lang's own method in the selected cases to
which he applies it. He devotes a chapter to the
mythology of Egypt, and pronounces the beast-
headed deities of that country to be survivals from
savage totemism. Now, if there is any one ancient
mythology the significance of which, owing to the
abundance of ancient materials, is absolutely trans-
parent, it is that of Egypt ; and here, if the totemistic
theory is correct, it ought to be easy to establish it.
But Mr. Renouf, following such excellent authorities
as De Rougé, Mariette, and Brugsch, has shown that
the early Egyptian religion was essentially elemental

and largely solar ; while the grosser and more corrupt elements, the polytheism and the beast-worship,
came in at a later day, gradually developing themselves down to the time of the Ptolemies. In the
earlier texts the deities are few, and not totemistic
but elemental. Osiris, Ra, Tum, and Horus are the
Sun in different aspects ; Nut and Seb are the
Heaven and the Earth, parents of the Sun ; Isis, the
bride of Osiris, is the Dawn ; Set is the Darkness,
Anubis the Twilight, and Thoth the Moon. Because
these deities, whose significance is clear, are represented under animal forms or symbols, Mr. Lang
contends that they were not elemental but totemistic.
But Mr. Renouf has in several cases been able to
explain how the animal representations originated.
Thus Seb was the earth ; but the word *seb* in
Egyptian signified also a goose, and hence the name
of the Earth-god was ideographically expressed by
the picture of a goose, which became the symbol of
the deity. For a similar reason Thoth was represented by an ibis. These symbols no more imply an
early totemism than the fish so often found pictured
in the Roman catacombs proves the totemistic origin
of Christian belief. The fish was a baptismal
symbol, and the word ἰχθύς was also an anagram
formulating the Christian creed. In other cases the
animal representations of Egyptian deities were
plainly symbols : like the lion of St. Mark, the eagle
of St. John, the cock of St. Peter ; or the lamb, the
dove, the hart, the peacock, the duck, and the fish
represented on the sixth century ambo in the

cathedral at Ravenna. These animal symbols might with as much reason be adduced to prove the origin of Christian belief in totemistic savagery as many of the Egyptian and Greek examples on which Mr. Lang relies."

When a reviewer quite misstates the ideas of his patient it is probable that the patient is partly to blame. I may have so written as to make my critic think that my opinions about the Egyptian religion were almost the very reverse of what I really hold. My reviewer says :—" In the earlier texts the deities are few, and not totemistic but elemental. Osiris, Ra, Tum, and Horus are the Sun in different aspects ; Nut and Seb are the Heaven and the Earth ; Isis, the bride of Osiris, is the Dawn ; Set is the Darkness. . . . Because these deities, whose significance is clear, are represented under animal forms or symbols, Mr. Lang contends that they are not elemental but totemistic." I never believed anything of the sort, and I trust that I never said anything of the sort. I do not feel sure that Isis is the Dawn ; I do not feel sure that Osiris was not a kind of Hades before he was identified with the Nocturnal Sun, and with many other aspects of nature. What I said is :—

"'In the oldest tombs, where the oldest writings are found, there are not many gods mentioned— there are Osiris, Horus, Thot, Seb, Nut, Hathor, Anubis, Apheru, and a couple more.'[1] Here was a stock of gods who remained in credit till 'the dog Anubis' fled from the Star of Bethlehem. Most of these deities bore birth-marks of the sky and of the tomb. If Osiris was 'the sun-god of Abydos,' he was also the murdered and mutilated culture-hero. If Hor or Horus was the sun at his height, he too had suffered despiteful usage from his enemies. Seb and Nut (named on the coffin of Mycerinus of the fourth dynasty in the British Museum) were our old friends the personal heaven and earth. Anubis, the jackal, was 'the lord of the grave,' and dead kings are worshipped no less than gods who were thought to have been dead kings. While certain gods, who re-tained permanent power, appear in the oldest monu-ments, sacred animals are also present from the first. The gods, in fact, of the earliest monuments were beasts. Here is one of the points in which a great alteration developed itself in the midst of Egyptian religion. Till the twelfth dynasty, when a god is mentioned (and in those very ancient remains gods are not mentioned often), 'he is represented by his animal, or with the name spelled out in hieroglyphs, often beside the bird or beast.'[2] 'The jackal stands for Anup (Anubis), the frog for Hekt, the baboon for Tahuti (Thoth). It is not till after Semitic

---

[1] Lieblein, *Egyptian Religion*, p. 7.
[2] Flinders Petrie, *Arts of Ancient Egypt*, p. 8.

influence had begun to work in the country that any figures of gods are found.' By 'figures of gods' are meant the later man-shaped or semi-man-shaped images, the hawk-headed, jackal-headed, and similar representations with which we are familiar in the museums. The change begins with the twelfth dynasty, but becomes most marked under the eighteenth."

Is this not a sufficient admission of the elemental character of many gods? Do I not say that these gods "bear birth-marks of the sky"? that two of them are "personal heaven and earth"? Are Osiris and Horus not regarded as sun-gods? Can I help it if, on the oldest monuments, they are figured by their beasts? Again, I have failed to explain my meaning if I have said that "the beast-headed deities of the country are survivals from savage totemism." What I mean is that (in many cases) the bestial head which Osiris or Amun Ra wears, in works of art, is a survival from totemism, not that an elemental god was originally totemistic. I pointed out that, in localities where a beast was specially adored, there a god with the head of that beast "finds the centre and chief holy place of his worship." I never dreamed of saying that Osiris, Ra, Tum, and Horus, Isis

and Set, were " not elemental but totemistic," as
the reviewer declares. I accepted (ii. 110) M.
Maspero's classification of the gods :—" The gods
of death and of the dead were Sokari, Isis and
Osiris, the young Horus and Nepthys. The elemental gods were Seb (Earth) and Nut (Heaven),
with others. Among solar deities are at once
recognised Ra, and others, but there was a strong
tendency to identify each of the gods with the
sun, especially to identify Osiris with the sun in
his nightly absence." I said that many of the
gods were represented, from various causes, with
bestial heads and so forth. But the reviewer
declares :—" Because these deities, whose significance is clear, are represented under animal
forms as symbols, Mr. Lang contends that they
are not elemental but totemistic." This is pretty
nearly the very reverse of what I do say. One
may state again, and afresh, one's opinion about
the religion of Egypt.

I believe that, as far back as Egyptian religion
can be traced, we find gods like Osiris, Nut, Isis,
Seb, gods of elements, gods of departments, and that
we also find the survivals of totemism in locally
worshipped beasts, and in the custom of represent-
ing gods by beasts on the monuments. I believe

that the elemental and departmental gods, in the general syncretism and muddle of schools, faiths, and politics, often wore each other's insignia, as kings and emperors wear the uniform of regiments in each other's service. These insignia, such as bestial heads, are often, to my mind, relics of totemism. The reviewer gives M. Le Page Renouf's idea that Thoth was merely represented by an ibis. He is piously careful *not* to quote M. Maspero :—" Whatever they may have worshipped in Thoth-Ibis, it was a bird, and not a hieroglyph, that the first worshippers of the ibis adored " (*Revue de l'Histoire des Religions*, vol. i.) The reviewer gives the opinions of De Rougé, Mariette, and Brugsch, who more or less agree with him. His readers must find out for themselves that Maspero, Meyer, Tiele, Perrot, Pietschmann, and Sayce are against him on the whole. When the reviewer brings in "the lion of St. Mark, the eagle of St. John," and so forth, to show that the "animal representations of Egyptian deities were plainly symbolical," he does not tell his readers that I have specially mentioned these very sacred Christian beasts as a warning against hasty generalisations about totemism. Why, the Evangelists, as I show, are occasionally beast-headed in art, and, as I have said, "we must not forget that repre- sentations of this kind in art may be only a fanciful kind of shorthand."

The science of religion can hardly be advanced by attributing to an opponent ideas which he does not hold, nor by quoting his adversaries while his "great allies" are carefully left in silence, nor by adducing, as opposed to his general theory, the very considerations which he has advanced to show that the theory must not be rashly pushed to extremes. But in these studies it is hard to make oneself understood by the partisans of opposite ideas. I believe that down to the time of Herodotus and Juvenal, when one nome worshipped a sacred beast and persecuted the beast of the neighbouring nome, and once a year solemnly sacrificed its own beast, *that* was a survival of totemism. I believe that when a departmental or elemental god wore a bestial head, that was in many cases a kind of com- pliment to the local sacred beast, who, again, had been a totem. But only an uneducated fanatic could fancy that the elemental gods had once been totems, or would deny that certain even of the sacred animals need never have been totems at all (Tiele, *Theolog. Tidjsch.*, twelfth year, p. 261). The object of the study of religion is to unweave the many threads that make its complicated pattern, not to maintain that all manifestations of faiths have the same source, whether it be totemism, or the worship of Ancestors, or worship of the Elements, or worship of Deities invented for the purpose of making them preside over this or that department—Weather, Love, War, Fire, or what not. As to the origin of a belief in gods, it lies far behind the period which we can investigate.

Had Herodotus been compelled to state his own theory of the origin of the religion he knew, perhaps he would have declared that the oldest form was the Pelasgian (ii. 52). " They gave no name nor by-name to any of the gods, for they had heard of none." He would, perhaps, have inferred that the Pelasgians acted as they did under a *sensus numinis ;* a variety of vague inferences from unrecorded and unanalysed impressions, all making for a belief in the Divine. To these worshippers came, from Egypt to Dodona, the notion that the gods had names, and the origin of the habit of naming them. The names themselves were "given by Homer and Hesiod," a very curious assertion. As for Herodotus himself, he plainly declares that "whence sprang each of the gods, and whether they all were from all eternity, and of what fashion they be, came to men's knowledge, as they say, but yesterday." To the knowledge of Herodotus these matters clearly never came at all. He is the most agnostic of religious, the most religious of agnostic men.

THE GOOD FAITH OF HERODOTUS.

THE good faith of Herodotus hath often been impugned, never more anxiously than by Professor Sayce in his "Ancient Empires of the East, Herodotus, i.–iii." (London, 1883 [1]). Professor Sayce decides that the greater part of

---

[1] No attempt is made here to discuss points of Egyptology, or Oriental lore, in which the author would make but a poor figure. Nor are questions of textual criticism and grammar raised. The object is merely to study the charges brought against Herodotus, which can be examined in the light of Herodotus himself, his character, purpose, and method. To intrude on the special studies of a learned critic would be mere impertinent sciolism. But we have all a right to read Herodotus.

what our author tells us about the history of Egypt, Babylonia, and Persia is really a " collection of *märchen*, or popular stories, current among the Greek loungers and half-caste dragomen on the skirts of the Persian Empire." Even if this be true, as Professor Sayce remarks, " for the student of folklore they are invaluable." Folklore is itself a branch of history—of the history of the human mind—and we may thank Herodotus for ἱστορίης ἀπόδεξις ἥδε. It is clear that *we* cannot blame him for collecting folklore. The question as to his good faith is not decided in the negative because he amassed traditions and legends. The real questions are, does Herodotus usually take *märchen* for historical facts, or does he merely give them for what they may be worth? And again, is he honest in his inquiry, and in his statements? As M. Maspero remarks, *Herodotus was not writing a history of Egypt.*[1] Herodotus merely tells us " the current legend in the streets of Memphis." Professor Sayce admits this—he admits that Herodotus is here the folklorist, not the historian—but the admission does not prevent him from criticising the most delightful narrator in the world much as

[1] *Contes Egyptiens*, p. xxxiii.

an unfriendly critic might treat Mr. Allan Quatermain.[1]

In his critic's opinion Herodotus "can see nothing but folly in the belief of his fore-fathers."[2] Yet he is more commonly charged with credulity, and is said to have "made demands upon the credulity" of his age.[3] Deserting the notion that, in his Egyptian traditional lore, Herodotus is merely the collector of *märchen*, his critic accuses him of "jealousy of others who had done what he thought he could himself do better," and of having a theory to maintain, "a philosophical, or, if the term is preferred, a theological theory, which was a combination of the old Greek belief in the doom that awaits hereditary guilt, and the artistic Greek conception of the golden mean." Why a man who "could see nothing but folly in the belief of his forefathers" should make false statements to buttress that very "old Greek belief" does not appear. But Professor Sayce attributes to Herodotus's pious care for a theory based on the "old Greek belief" (which Hero-

---

[1] I am unable to verify the criticism attributed to Lucian. *Vera. Hist.* ii. 42.
[2] *Op. cit.* p. 33, *note* 4.　　　[3] Page xiii.

dotus, ex hypothesi, "thought folly") his account, for example, of the dreams that preceded the expedition of Xerxes. That expedition "has to be preceded by dreams."[1] Now it does not seem bigoted to hint that these are not coherent charges. If Herodotus, like Homer, believed that the gods indicated coming events by dreams, then he saw a good deal besides "folly" in the "belief of his forefathers." He might, therefore, well record the stories of these visions, without being prompted by mere desire to uphold a theory. Again, if the tales were current, they came within the very province of Herodotus as defined by M. Maspero: "Il nous apprend ce qu'on disait dans les rues de" Susa. Thus we can scarcely admit, so far, that any point has been made against the good faith or the old Greek piety of Herodotus.

As to the various dates at which the Histories of Herodotus were published, as to the number of contemporary "editions" which it "underwent," the questions may provoke the learned discussion of critics, but are scarcely capable of being solved. What was "an edition" in these early days; what was the mode of publication?

[1] Page xvi.

For matters of fact Herodotus relies, as Professor Sayce shows, on such authorities as could
then be found. It is certain that he was unable
to read the Egyptian inscriptions. Whether he
could tell a "forged Cadmeian" from a genuine
inscription seems beyond our means to discern,
as we have not the said Cadmeian or semi-
Phœnician inscriptions before us. But it is
extremely interesting, if it is true, that even in
or before the period of Herodotus the clergy of
Thebes were archæologists enough to be able to
counterfeit very archaic writing.[1] Herodotus
is discussing the date of writing in Greece. The
Cadmeian or Phœnician characters he saw in the
tripods at Thebes were "mainly like the Ionian."
One tripod pretended to be dedicated by Amphi-
tryon, another by Hippocoon, a contemporary of
Laius. There *may* have been early Thebans so
named, or the inscriptions *may* have been written
at an early period to support that belief. In any
case Herodotus is merely speaking of the characters which, though "Cadmeian," were already
very like Ionian letters. He does not say,
though probably enough he believed, that the
tripods had actually been dedicated by the

[1] The passage is v. 59.

father of Heracles. The motive for forgery may have existed, but is not very apparent, unless it were merely to demonstrate the antiquity of the shrine.

Oracles, traditions, eye-witnesses, priests (or rather half-caste dragomen, whom Herodotus would so naturally mistake for priests), poets, foreign authors ("in cribs," as Colonel Newcome says), and Greek predecessors in prose, were among the sources of Herodotus. The list is long. But Professor Sayce, rather unkindly, finds traces of the "malignity" of Herodotus even in his quotations. He cites no Greek prose writer by name but Hecatæus, and differs from *him*. As to Sophocles, "his tragedies had formed no part of the school education of Herodotus ; he had learned no passages from them, and was consequently unable to quote from them." But Mr. Swinburne formed no part of my school education, nor indeed did the *Border Minstrelsy.* Yet, without boasting, I could quote Mr. Swinburne and the ballads for an hour by Shrewsbury clock.

Probably the poetic knowledge of Herodotus was not limited by the "rep" he learned at school. It is also urged that he did not quote

Sophocles, because, as he was the "fashionable tragedian," "knowledge of a poet about whom every one was talking did not bring with it the same reputation of learning as a knowledge of prehistoric worthies like Musæus and Bacis." But if "every one was talking" about Sophocles, Herodotus must have been lonely in his ignorance if he could not quote him. It may be fancied, too, that Musæus and Bacis were not less familiar to Greeks than Thomas the Rhymer's prophecies to the Scotch borderers of a hundred years ago, and of earlier times. In that case a man might quote them without ostentation of learning.

We are discussing the good faith of Herodotus. Is it at all seriously disparaged by such arguments as these? Nay, do not such arguments display a certain prejudice in the mind of his critic? If this prejudice appears to exist, we may discount some of the other charges, for example, as to earlier prose writers, that Herodotus's "chief aim was to use their materials without letting the fact be known." We, too, are, and confess to being, prejudiced—prejudiced, not by ill-will, but by gratitude to Herodotus. We believe that he was a gentleman and a good man.

There is an age in the evolution of literature—
an age surviving in the East, when each man
writes, uses, and annexes as matter of custom
the compilations of his predecessors. M. Renan
makes this remark in his Biblical criticism.
Herodotus may have been just emerging from
this artless period of recognised plagiarism. I
am pleading, as it were, for the favourable con-
sideration of a very old friend. Professor Sayce
remarks, on the other side, that "the passport
to fame among the Greek-reading public of the
age of Herodotus was the affectation of novelty
and contemptuous criticism of older writers."
Perhaps the reading public of to-day may prefer
the same credentials. But I would not pass
"contemptuous criticism on" a writer so old as
Herodotus. And it is curious that the contemporary critics of our Homer were, according to
that hypothesis, so careful to forge archaisms, if
the way to popularity was not through antiquity
but through novelty. As to Hecatæus, from
whom Herodotus is here said to have stolen, it
is not so certain that the fragments attributed to
him are not a late *pastiche* from Herodotus.[1]
The passage in which Porphyry accuses Herodo-

---

[1] *Edinburgh Review*, 1884, p. 541.

tus of stealing his phœnix, hippopotamus, and crocodile hunt from Hecatæus is in Eusebius.[1] Eusebius is retorting on his opponents the foolish and futile charge of " plagiarism." " Plagiarists yourselves, as Porphyry shows," he cries, and then quotes a long black calendar, including Herodotus. But even if Herodotus gave the same account as Hecatæus of certain bits of folk-lore, or current waterside talk, βραχία παραποιήσας, that proves nothing. Nobody denies that Hecatæus and Herodotus were both in Egypt at nearly the same time. The stories of the phœnix and the crocodile catching, which were told to one would be told to the other, and both might repeat them in much the same way. Any European traveller at Amo-rosiky, in Madagascar, may hear the *conte* which explains why a clan of Betsunarakas do not eat beef, and may repeat, almost in the same words as my friend Commander Haggard, the story of "The Crocodile in Love." Yet neither European would have plagiarised from the other. As Professor Sayce writes of " the mystical Phœnix (*bennu*), which brings the ashes of its former self to Heliopolis every five

[1] *Præp. Evan.,* x. 3.

hundred years," he surely must perceive that the tale was current, and might have been told in similar terms, and in similar terms reported, without any plagiarism, both by Herodotus and Hecatæus. Indeed, Herodotus (ii. 73) expressly gives the tale as a story of the people of Heliopolis, which he declined to believe. Is it credible that he plagiarised a mere anecdote which he declines to accept for more than a *märchen?* But Professor Sayce declares that "even in the ancient world it was notorious that he had stolen" the fable. The "notoriety" is the gossip of Porphyry, in a late age of forgeries.

We like not Bardolph's security. The critic himself admits (p. xxiii.) that Herodotus may have taken a piece of folk-lore "from the same source" as Charon took his. Why should we not be as lenient in the case of the Phœnix? As for Dr. Smith's Classical Dictionary, that learned authority declares the charge of plagiarism brought by Porphyry to be "wholly without foundation."

His critic is so hard on poor Herodotus, that one is obliged to fight him point by point. He desires to show the malignity of Herodotus.

Now (iii. 15) the traveller says he could find no certain eye-witness to tell him about the sea on the North of Europe, "though I did my best" (τοῦτο μελετῶν): "obgleich ich Mühe darauf ver-wandte" (Stein). Professor Sayce remarks that Herodotus, "when he is trying to disparage his predecessors, ostentatiously asserts it was his invariable rule to consult eye-witnesses." These charges of disparagement and ostentation are based on this passage (iii. 15), where Herodotus says nothing about "invariable rules" at all, but merely remarks that he did his best to find an eye-witness in one given case. It is not the good faith of Herodotus that suffers from this accusation, unless τοῦτο μελετῶν means, "as I make my invariable rule." But I am not disposed to pronounce for the correctness of this translation.

Mr. Sayce declares that Herodotus, "to judge from the way he writes, must have been a marvellous linguist, being able to converse freely with Egyptians, Phœnicians, Arabians, Carthaginians, Babylonians, Skythians, Tau-rians, Kolkhians, Thrakians, Karians, Kaunians, and Persians."

Does Herodotus tell us, or imply, that he

talked in all these languages? Were there not "Dragomen"? May not the foreigners have known Greek? As to *Phœnicians* (ii. 44), he conversed with "the priests of the god at Tyre." He does not say he conversed in Phœnician. As Mr. Sayce thinks that Herodotus's Egyptian priests were often Dragomen, he might make a similar allowance in Phœnicia. *Carthaginians* (iv. 43): Herodotus says not a word about conversing with them. Μετὰ δὲ Καρχηδόνιοί εἰσι οἱ λέγοντες (*sc.* γνῶναι αὐτήν, Stein). I confess I am at a loss to imagine how this can be regarded as a statement of Herodotus, that he could converse with Carthaginians. Nor is it anything but likely that the mercantile folk of Carthage could speak Greek. *Arabians* (ii. 108): "The Arabians also tell this tale," namely that, except for a providential arrangement, serpents would overrun the land. Who is boasting of being able to talk with Arabians? If I say "there is a Basque legend that the devil could not learn Basque," am I professing to be a greater linguist than the devil? *Babylonians* (i. 18 1.): "As the Chaldæans say," a woman sleeps with the god. Would any one "judge, from the way in which he writes," that Herodotus was here asserting his power of conversing in Chaldæan? "The priests assert," he remarks, and never pretends that they spoke to him in their own tongue, and that he understood them. *Scythians* (iv. 5) : "As the Scythians say, theirs is the youngest of peoples," and so forth. A man can speak only for himself; but it certainly never occurred to me that, in these and the similar texts, Herodotus was claiming credit as a linguist. About the Colchians and Egyptians he does say that "their tongues are alike," and here he probably went beyond his scope, and judged merely from unfamiliar sounds, which, he fancied, resembled each other. Professor Sayce adds a note on "his remark that Egyptian resembled the chattering of birds" (ii. 57). What Herodotus *does* say is that some Egyptian women seemed to the people of Dodona to chatter like birds. It does not appear that Herodotus gives any opinion of his own as to the sound of the Egyptian language. The talking doves of Dodona are merely ancestors in folklore of the birds of ballads—

"There cam' a bird frae Weary's Well,
On water for to dine "—

and talking doves and nightingales are common

in French *Volks-lieder.*[1] The argument that Herodotus did not know the name of Osiris, because he often declines to mention him, is Wiedemann's. Professor Sayce puts it : "Herodotus or his authorities had not caught the name when taking notes; but, instead of confessing the fact, the father of history deliberately deceives his readers." Can any one really doubt the extreme reverence of Herodotus? Are all his veilings of the sacred chapters he knows mere concealments of ignorance? For example, when he says (ii. 45), "Gods and heroes be merciful to me for speaking thus!" When he speaks of Osiris, where he thinks fit to name him (ii. 48), he styles him Dionysus. In ii. 170 he will not name the god, because the god's *tomb* is in question. In fact, he conceals the name in places where the Death, Burial, and Lament for the Deity have to be mentioned, just as Plutarch, in a later age, will not tell all he knows on such subjects. He approaches with reverence a topic so awful as the slaying of a god.

---

[1] P. 180, note 2. The critic admits that it was "the Dodona people" who could not distinguish between the Egyptian language and the chirping of doves—a strange way of putting what Herodotus really says.

Εἰσὶ δὲ καὶ αἱ ταφαὶ τοῦ οὐκ ὅσιον ποιεῦμαι ἐπὶ τοιούτῳ πρήγματι ἐξαγορεύειν τοὔνομα (ii. 170).

" Yet elsewhere Herodotus has no scruple about mentioning Osiris under his Greek title, Dionysus ! "

Then how could he be ignorant of the Greek title? It is plain that he only abstained from using the god's name when he had to touch on the Divine death and funeral rites. This is reverence, not fraudulent ignorance.

So, at least, we naturally understand it. But, if we find the good faith of Herodotus clear, and if theories of dishonesty and ignorance seem forced, enough has been said. The present writer has never been in Egypt, and cannot estimate the value of attacks on the local knowledge of Herodotus. If it is a question of the character of Herodotus, has that character suffered at all from the charges we have examined? If not, we are well content. For this is an old friend, and we are satisfied if the evidence that seeks to prove him a vain, mendacious, jealous plagiarist has been found wanting. He is no man of modern science, no philologist, no authority on ancient Egyptian monuments. He is a Greek, reverent, religious, curious, yet far from being idly credulous; he is a traveller, a collector of traditions, an admirable writer, though "his speculations on philology and ethnology are never very profound."

It is intelligible that writers of an erudite age, whose speculations are always very profound, should quarrel with Herodotus, because he certainly was entirely ignorant of much that they know. He did not pass the limitations of his own country and his own time. But, take him for all he was, and all he claimed to be, and a pleasanter Worthy than Herodotus, a writer more kindly, truthful, pious, and entertaining, is not to be found in the greatest literature of the world. He was not a modern philologist, or Egyptologist. But one is puzzled to understand how this inevitable defect can be so unpardonable as to make him appear, in the eyes of learning, a liar, a boaster, and a thief.

HERODOTUS

HIS SECOND BOOK ENTITULED
EUTERPE.

FTER the death of the moſt noble
and vertuous King *Cyrus,* there
fucceeded him in the empyre a
fon of his, named *Cambyſes,* born
of *Caſſandana* daughter to *Phar-*
naſphus, who dying long tyme before the king
hir ſpouſe, was greatly bewayled by him, and his
whole empyre. The younge prince *Cambyſes*
makinge none other accounte of the *Iones,* then of
his lawfull feruants left him by the due right and
title of inheritaunce, went in expedition againſt
the *Ægyptians,* preparing an army as well out
of other countreys as alſo out of the regions
and borders of *Greece,* which were under his
gouernment. The *Ægyptians* before ſuch time
as *Pſammetichus* held the ſupremicy, thought
them

them felues to haue bene the firft and mofte
auncient people of the world. This king in time
of his raigne and gouernaunce in *Ægypt,* for the
great defire hee had to know by what people
the earth was firft inhabited wrought an experience whereby the *Ægyptians* were broughte
to thinke that the *Phrygians* were the moft old
and auncient people of the earth, and them felues
to be nexte in antiquity to them. For *Pfammetichus* by all meanes indeuouringe to know
who they were that firft and before al others
came into the world, finding himfelfe hardly
fatisfied with ought he could heare : pra&ifed a
deuife and feate of his owne braine. Two young
infants borne of bafe parentes, hee gaue to his
Sheepheard to bring up and nourifh in this
maner. He gaue comaundement that no man
in their prefence or hearing fhould fpeake one
word : but that being alone in a folitary and
deferte cabyne farre from all company, they
fhould haue milke and other foode brought and
myniftred to them in due and conuenient time.
Which thinges were done and commaunded by
him, to the intent that when they left of
their childifh cries and began to prattle and
fpeake plainly, he might know what fpeach and
language they would firft ufe : which in proceffe
of time fell out and happened accordingly. For
being

being of the age of two yeares, it chaunced that
the fheepheard (who was their Nourice and
bringer up) approching neere to the dore of the
Cottage and entering in, both the little brats
fprawling at his feete, and ftretching forth It were a
their hands, cryed thus: *Beccos, Beccos :* which queftion if a
man fhould
at the firft hearing, the Paftour noted only and bee taught
no language,
made no words: but perceyuing him felfe al- in what
tongue hee
wayes faluted after one fort : and that euermore would
fpeake.
at his entraunce the children fpake the fame word,
the matter was opened to the king : at whofe
comaundement he brought the children and deliuered them up into his hands : whom when
Pfammetichus alfo himfelfe had heard to chat in
the fame maner, he made curioufe fearch what
people ufed the word *Beccos* in their language,
and in what meaning they toke it.   Whereby he
came to know that the word was accuftomably
ufed by the people of *Phrygia* to fignifie bread.
For which caufe the *Ægyptians* came into opinion, that the *Phrygians* were of greater time
and longer continuance then them fêlues. Of all
which matter, and ˙the maner of doing thereof,
I was credibly informed by the prieftes of the
god *Vulcane*, abiding at *Memphis*.   Howbeit
many fond fables are recited by the *Grecian*
writers, that *Pfammetichus* geuing the children
to certaine women of the country to fucke and
bring

bring up, cauſed their tongues to bee cut out that they might not ſpeake to them. Thus much was rehearſed by them of the trayning up and education of the infants. Many other things alſo were told me by the holy and religious Chaplaynes of the god *Vulcane*, with whom I had often conference at *Memphis*.

Moreouer, for the ſame occaſion I toke a iourney to *Thebs* and *Heliopolis*, which is to wit, the city of the *Sunne*, to the end I might ſee whether they would iumpe all in one tale and agree together. For the *Heliopolitans* are ſayd to bee the moſt prudent and witty people of all the *Ægyptians*. Notwithſtanding of diuine and heauenly matters, as touching their gods, loke what they told me I am purpoſed to conceale, ſaue onely their names, which are manifeſtly knowne of all men : of other matters I meane to keepe ſilence, vnleſſe by the courſe of the Hyſtory I ſhall perforce bee broughte into a narration of the ſame. In all their talke of mortall and humane affayres, they did rightly accord and conſent one with an other : ſaying this : that the *Ægyptians* firſt of all others found out the circuite and compaſſe of the yeare, deuiding the ſame into 12 feuerall moneths according to the courſe and motion of the ſtarres : making (in my fancy) a better computation

Heliopolis the city of the Sunne.

The wiſeſt people in Ægypt.

The 12 monethes of the yeare firſt found out by the Ægyptians.

computation of the time then the *Grecians*
doe, which are driuen euery thirde yeare to
adde certaine dayes to fome one moneth,
whereby the yeares may fall euen and become
of a iuft compaffe. Contrarywife, the *Ægyptians*
to three hundred dayes which they parte and
diftribute into twelue moneths, making addition
of fiue odde dayes, caufe the circle and courfe of
their yeares to fall out equally and alwayes a
like. In like maner the *Ægyptians* first inuented
and ufed the furnames of the twelue gods: which
the *Grecians* borowed and drew from them.
The felfe fame were the firft founders of Aulters,
Images, and Temples to the gods: by whom
alfo chiefly were carued the pictures of beafts
and other creatures in ftone, which thing for
the moft parte they proue and confirme by lawfull teftimonyes and good authority: to this they
ad befides that the firft king that ever raygned
was named *Menes*, under whofe gouernaunce all
the lande of *Ægypt* except the prouince of
Theles was wholly couered and ouerwhelmed
with water, and that no parte of the ground
which lyes aboue the poole called *Myris* was
then to be fene: into which poole from the fea
is 7. dayes fayling. And truly as concerning the
country they feemed to fpeake truth. For it is
euident to all men (who hauing neuer heard
thereof

The names of the 12 gods, Aulters, Images, and Temples, inuented by the Ægyptians.

Menes the firft kinge that euer raygned.

Ægypte for the moft parte couered with water.

thereof doe but onely beholde it) how that parte
of *Ægypt* whereat the *Grecians* are wont to
arryue is gayned ground, and as it were the gyft
of the ryuer. Likwife all the land aboue the
poole for the fpace of three dayes fayleing;
whereof notwithftanding they fpake nothing at
all. Befides, there is another thing from whence
no fmale profe may be borowed: to wit, the
very nature and quality of the *Ægyptian* foile:
which is fuch that being in voyage towards
Ægypt, after you come within one dayes fayling
of the lande, at euery founde with the plummet,
you fhall bringe uppe great ftore of mud and
noyfome filth, euen in fuch place as the water is
eleuen ells in depth: whereby it is manyfeft
that fo farre the ground was caft uppe and left
bare by the waters. The length of *Ægypt* by
the fea coafte is 423 miles and a halfe: according to our lymitation which is from the coafte of
Plynthines, to the poole named *Sellonis*, where-
unto reacheth an ende of the great mountayne
Caſſius: on this fide therefore *Ægypte* is fixety
fcheanes, which conteyne the number of myles
before mentioned. For with the *Ægyptians*
fuch as are flenderly landed, meafure their ground
by paces, they which haue more, by furlongs,
unto whom very much is allotted, by the *Perfian*
myle named *Parafanga:* laftly fuch as in large
and

The maner
of the Ægyp-
tians meu-
fures.

and ample poffeffions exceede the reft, meete
their territory by *Schœnes*. The meafure *Para-*
fanga contayneth thirty furlongs, the *Schœne*
threefcore, whereby it cometh to paffe that the
lande of *Ægypt* along the fea is 3600. furlongs,
from this parte towarde the citie *Heliopolis* and
the middle region : *Ægypt* is very wyde and
broade a playne and champion countrey, defti-
tute of waters, yet very flimie and full of mudde.
The iourney from the fea to *Heliopolis* by the
higher parte of the region, is welnigh of the
fame length with that way, which at *Athens*
leadeth from the aulter of the twelve gods to
Pifa, and the palace of *Iupiter Olympius*, betwene which two wayes by iuft computation can
hardly bee founde more than fifteene furlonges
difference : for the diftaunce betwene *Athens*
and *Pifa* is fuppofed to want of 1500 furlongs,
fiftene, which number in the other of *Ægypt* is
ful, complet, and perfit : trauayling from *Heliopolis* by the hills you fhall finde *Ægypt* to be
ftraight and narrowe compaffed, banked on the
one fide by a mighty hill of *Arabia*, reachinge
from the North towardes the South which by
degrees waxeth higher and higher, and beareth
upwards toward the redd fea. In this mountayne are fundry quaries out of the which the
people of *Ægypte* hewed their ftone to builde
the

the *Pyramides* at *Memphis :* one this fide, the
hill draweth and wyndeth it felfe towarde thofe
places whereof we fpake before. The felf fame
mountayne hath another courfe from the Eafte
to the Wefte ftretching fo farre in length as a
man may trauayle in two monethes : the Eafte
ende hereof yeldeth frankincenfe in great aboun-
daunce : likewife one the other fide of *Ægypt*
which lyeth towardes *Africa,* there runneth
another ftony hill, wherein are builte certayne
Pyramedes very full of grauell and groffe Sande,
like unto that parte of the *Arabian* hill that
beareth toward the South : fo that from *Helyo-
polis* the wayes are very narrow not paffing foure
dayes courfe by Sea.

A moun-
taine.

The fpace betwene the mountaynes is champion ground, being in the narroweft place not
aboue two hundred furlongs from the one hill to
the other : hauing paffed this ftraight, *Ægypt*
openeth into a large and ample wideneffe ex-
tendinge it felfe in great breadth : fuch is the
maner and fituation of the countrey.

Furthermore, from *Heliopolis* to *Thebs* is nyne
dayes iourney by water, being feuered from each
other in diftance of place foure thowfand eight
hundred and fixty furlongs, which amounteth to
the number of foure fcore and one *fchænes ;* of
the furlongs aforefayd, three thowfand and fixe
hundred

hundred lye to the fea, as wee declared before:
Now from the fea coafte to the city *Thebs* are
6120 furlonges of playne ground, and from
Thebs to the city *Elephantina*, 820. Of all the
region and countrey of *Ægypt* whereof we
haue fpoken the moft parte is borowed ground,
wherein the waters heretofore haue had their
courfe : for all the whole bottome which lyeth
betwene the two mountaines aboue the city
Memphis feemeth to haue bene a narrow fea,
much like unto thofe places that lye about
Ilium, Teuthrania, Ephefus, and the playne of
Meander: if it be not amiffe to bring fmale
things in comparifon with greater matters : forafmuch as none of thofe ryuers which held their
paffage in the places forenamed, are worthy to
be mentioned where any one of the feuen
ftreames of *Nylus* are brought into talke : there The ftrange
be alfo other floudes not comparable in bigneffe certayne
to *Nilus,* which haue wrought ftraunge effectes ryuers.
and wonderfull thinges in the places where
they haue runne amongft whom is the famous
ryuer *Achelous,* which flowing through *Acar-*
nania into the fea of the Iles *Echinades,* hath
joyned the halfe parte of the Iles to the mayne
and continent. In the countrey of *Aralia,*
not far from *Ægypt* there is a certaine arme
or bofome of the fea, hauing a breach and
iffue

iffue out of the red fea, the length whereof
beginning at the end of the angle or creeke and
continuing to the wyde mayne, is foure dayes
fayle: the breadth eafy to be cut ouer in halfe a
day: in this narrow fea the waters ebbe and flow,
raging and roaring exceedingly againft a forde
or fhalow place, wherat the ftreame beateth with
great violence: fuch a like creeke I fuppofe to
haue bene in former ages in the lande of *Ægypte*,
which brake out from the North fea, and continued his courfe towards *Æthyopia :* like as
alfo the *Arabian* fea (whereof we haue fpoken)
floweth from the fouth waters, towards the
coafts of *Syria*, both which ftraights welnigh
in their furtheft corners concur and meete together being feparated by no great diftaunce of
ground : were it then that the ryuer *Nilus* fhould
make a vent, and fhed it felfe into the narrow
fea of *Arabia*, what might hinder, but that in
200000 yeares, by the continuall and daily courfe
of the ryuer, the creeke of the falt waters fhould
be cleane altered and become dry: for I think it
poffible, if in 10000 yeares before me, fundry
ryuers haue changed their courfes and left the
ground dry whereas firft they ran : an arme of
the fea alfo much greater than that may bee
dryuen befides his naturall bofome, efpecially by
the force of fo great a ftreame as the riuer *Nilus*,

by

by whom diuerfe things of greater admiration
haue bene brought to paffe. The reporte therefore which they gaue of the foyle I was eafely By what
brought to beleue, afwel for that the country it proofes the
felfe bringeth credite to the beholders, as alfo that Ægypt is
in the very hills and mountaynes of the region haue bene
are found a multitude of fhel fifhes, the earth waters
likewife fweating out a certaine falt and brynifhe
humour, which doth corrupt and eate the *Pyramides*. Agayne, it is in no point like to any of
the countryes that lye next vnto it, neither to
Arabia, Lybia, nor *Syria*, (for the *Syrians* inhabite the fea coafte of *Arabia*) being of a blacke
and brittle moulde, which cometh to paffe by
the greate ftore of mudde and flimy matter
which the ryuer beinge a flote bringeth out of
Æthyopia into the lande of the *Ægyptians*.
The earth of *Lybia* is much more redde and fandy
underneath. The moulde of *Arabia* and *Syria*
drawe neere to a fatte and battle claye, beynge
vnder grounde very rockye and full of ftone.

Lykewyfe, for proofe that the Region in tyme
paft was watery ground the priefts alleadged
how in the time of kinge *Myris* his raygne the
floud aryfing to the heighth of 8 cubits watered
the whole countrey of *Ægypte* lying beneath
Memphis, fcarfe 900 yeares being paft and expired fince the death and deceafe of *Myris*:
whereas

whereas at thefe dayes vnleffe it fwell and increafe 15 or 16 cubits high, it cometh not at all

In Ægypt
it neuer
rayneth,
but their
lande is
watered by
the ouer-
flowe of
Nilus.

into that coaft, which aforefaid coaft, if accordingly to the fall of the riuer it grow ftill in lofty-
neffe and become higher, the earth receyuinge
no moyfture by the floude, I feare the *Ægyp-*
tians themfelues that dwell beneath the lake
Myris both other, and alfo the inhabitants of
the lande of *Delta*, will euermore be annoyed
with the fame plague and inconuenience, whych
the *Gretians* (by their accounte) are fometimes
like to abyde. For the people of *Ægypt* hearing
that the whole countrey of *Greece* was moyftned
and watered by the feafonable fall of rayne and
fhowers, and not by floudes and ryuers lyke vnto
their owne: they prophecy that the day would
come, when as the *Greekes* being deceyued of
their hope would all pearifhe through famine
and hunger: meaning that if the gods did not
vouchfafe to fend them raine in due feafon, from
whome alone they haue their moyfture, the
whole nation fhoulde goe to wracke for want of
fuftenaunce. Thus farre it pleafed them to
defcant of the fortune of *Greece*. Let us nowe
confider in what eftate and condition they ftand
them felues if then (as we fayd before) the lowe
countrey of *Memphis* (for in thefe is the gayne
and increafe of grounde feene) waxe and aug-
ment

ment accordingely as in former times, our
friendes of *Ægypt* fhall fhew us the way, what
it is to be famifhed and dye by hunger: if
neyther theyr land be moyftened by the fweete
and timely fhowres of rayne, nor by the fwelling
and ryfing of the riuer. For as now, they haue The maner
an efpeciall aduauntage afwell of all men els, amongft the
as of the reft of their countreymen that dwell Ægyptians.
higher, in that they receiue the fruite and increafe of the ground without eyther tilling or
weeding the earth, or doing ought els belonging
to hufbandry: wherefore immediately after the
ryfeing of the waters, the earth being moyfte and
fupple, and the ryuer returned agayne to his
olde courfe, they fowe and fcatter their feede
every one upon his own grounde and territory: wherinto hauing driuen great heards of
Swine that roote and tread the grayne and
moulds together, they ftay till the time of Hogs be
harveft, attending the increafe and gaine of hufbands in
their feede. Being full growne and ripened, the worft in
they fend in their hogges afrefh to muzle and England.
ftampe the corne from out the eares, which done,
they fweepe it together, and gather it. If we
follow the opinion of the people of *Ionia*, as
touching the land of *Ægypt*, who affirme, that A confuta-
the true countrey of *Aegypt* is in very deede opinion
nothing elfe faue the prouince of *Delta* (which concerning
taketh Aegypt.

taketh his name of the watchtowre or Caftle of
efpiall made by *Perfeus*) teftifying befides, that
by the fea coaft to the falt waters of *Pelufium*, it
ftretcheth forty fcheanes in length, and reacheth
from the fea toward the hart of the region, to
the city of the *Cercafians* (neere vnto which
the riuer *Nilus* parteth it felfe into two feueral
mouthes, the one whereof is called *Pelufium*,
the other *Canobus*) and that all the other partes
of *Aegypt* are belonging to *Arabia* and *Africa*,
we might very well inferre and prooue heereof,
that the countrey of *Aegypt* in former times was
none at all.　For the land of *Delta* (as they fay,
and we eafily beleeue) was grounde left voyde
and naked by the water, and that of late yeares
alfo and not long ago: wherefore if they had no
countrey at all, what caufed them fo curioufly to
labour in the fearching out and blazing of their
auncienty, fuppofing themfelues to be the chiefe
of all people, the knowledge and intelligence
whereof, was not worth the two yeares triall
and experiment which they wrought in the
children.　I my felfe am fully perfwaded, that
the *Aegyptians* tooke not their beginning together with the place of *Delta*, but were alwayes
fince the firft beginning and originall of man-
kinde, whofe countrey gayning ground, and increafing by the chaunge and alteration of the
riuer,

riuer, many of them went downe from the high
countrey, and inhabited the low places, for which
caufe, the City *Thebes*, and the countrey belonging thereto, was heeretofore called *Aegypt*, the
circuite and compaffe whereof is 6120 furlongs.
Be it fo then that our opinion accord and con-
fent wyth truth, the *Græcian* writers are in a
wrong boxe, but if they fpeake truely, yet in
other matters they recken without theyr hofte,
making but three partes of the whole earth,
Europa, *Afia*, and *Africa*: whereas of neceffity
Delta in *Aegypt* fhould be accounted for the
fourth: fithens by their owne bookes it is
neyther ioyned with *Afia*, nor yet with *Africa*.
For by this account, it is not the riuer *Nilus*
that diuides *Afia* from *Africa*, which at the
poynt and fharpe angle of *Delta*, cutting it felfe
into two fundry ftreames, that which lyes in the
middes fhould equally pertayne both to *Afia* and
Africa. But to leaue the iudgement and opinion
of the *Greekes*, we fay and affyrme, that all that
countrey is rightly tearmed *Aegypt*, whiche is
held and poffeffed by the *Aegyptians*, euen as
alfo we make no doubt to call thofe places
Cilicia and *Affyria* where the *Cilicians* and
Affyrians do dwell. In like manner, according
to truth, *Afia* and *Africa* are diffeuered and parted
betweene themfelues by none other borders, then

by

by the limits and boundes of *Aegypt.* Howbeit, if we followe the *Græcians*, all *Aegypt* (beginning at the places called *Catadupæ* and the city *Elephantina*) is to be diuided into two partes, which draw their names of the regions wherevnto they are adioyned, the one belonging to

The courfe of the riuer Nilus. *Africa*, the other to *Afia.* For the riuer *Nilus* taking his beginning from the *Catadupæ* fo called, and flowing through the middes of *Aegypt*, breaketh into the fea, running in one ftreame til it come to the city of the *Cercafians*, and afterwards feuering it felfe into three fundry

The names of the chanels of Nilus: Pelufium, Canobus. chanels. The firft of thefe chanels turneth to the Eaft, and is called *Pelufium*, the fecond *Canobus*, the third ftreame flowing directly in a ftraight line, kepeth this courfe, firft of all fcouring through the upper coaftes of the countrey, it beateth full upon the point of *Delta*, through the middeft whereof, it hath a ftraight and direct ftreame euen vnto the fea, being the fayreft and moft famous of all the reft of the chanels, and is

Sebennyticum. called *Sebennyticum.* From this ftreame are deriued two other armes alfo, leading to the falt

Saiticum. Menedefium. Bolbitinum. Bucolicum. waters, the one being called *Saiticum*, the other *Mendefium.* For as touching thofe braunches and ftreames of *Nilus*, which they tearme *Bolbitinum* and *Bucolicum*, they are not naturally made by courfe of the water, but drawne out

and

and digged by the labour of men. I followe not the fantafies of mine owne brayne, nor imagine any thing of my felfe, for that the countrey of *Aegypt* is so wyde, and of fuch amplitude as we haue defcribed it, I appeale to the oracle of the god *Hammon* which came into my minde, beeyng in ftudy and meditation about thefe matters.

The people of the two cities *Mœrea* and *Apia* that inhabite the borders of *Aegypt* next vnto *Africa*, efteeming themfelues to be of the linage and nation of the *Africans*, not of the Aegyptians, became weary of their ceremonies and religion, and would no longer abfteyne from the flefhe of kyne and feamale cattell, as the reft of the *Aegyptians* did, they fent therefore to the prophecy of *Hammon*, denying themfelues to be of *Aegypt*, becaufe they dwelt not within the compaffe of *Delta*, neither agreed with them in any thing, wherefore they defired the god that it might be lawful for them without reftraint to tafte of all meates indifferently : but the oracle forbade them fo to do, fhewing how all that region was iuftly accounted *Aegypt* which the waters of *Nilus* ouerranne and couered, adding heereto all thofe people that dwelling beneath the city *Elephantina*, dranke of the water of the fame floud. This aunfwere was giuen them by the

A ftory touching the defcription of Ægypt.

An oracle in Afrike.

B

the oracle. Nowe it is meete wee know, that *Nilus* at what time it rifeth aboue the banckes, ouerfloweth not *Delta* alone, but all the countrey next vnto *Africa*, and likewife the other fide adioyning to *Aralia*, couering the earth on both partes the fpace of two dayes iourney or there-about.

As touching the nature of the riuer *Nilus*, I could not bee fatisfyed either by the priefts, or by any other, being alwayes very willing and defirous to heare fomething thereof, firft, what the caufe might be that growing to fo great increafe, it fhould drowne and ouergo the whole countrey, beginning to fwell the eyght day before the kalends of July, and continuing aflote an hundred daies, after which time, in the like number of dayes it falleth agayne, flowyng within the compaffe of hys owne banckes tyll the nexte approch of July.

Of the caufes of thefe thynges the people of *Aegypt* were ignoraunte themfelues, not able to tell mee anye thyng whether *Nilus* had any proper and peculiar vertue different from the nature of other flouds. About which matters being very inquifitiue, mooued with defire of knowledge, I demaunded moreouer the reafon and occafion why this ftreame of all others neuer fent foorth any mifte or vapour, fuch as

are

Marginal notes:

How much of the lande of Nilus ouerfloweth.

The caufe and time of the rifing of the riuer.

Nilus fendeth foorth no mifte.

are commonly feene to afcend and rife from the
waters, but heerein alfo I was fayne to neftle in
mine owne ignorance, defiring to be lead of
thofe that were as blind as my felfe. Howbeit,
certayne *Græcian* wryters thinking to purchafe
the price and prayfe of wit, haue gone about to
difcourfe of *Nilus*, and fet downe their iudge- A refutation
of the
ment of the nature thereof, who are found to Grecians as
touching
varry and diffent in three fundry opinions, two the fame
things.
of the which I fuppofe not worth the naming,
but onely to giue the reader intelligence how
ridiculous they are. The firft is, that the ouer-
flow of *Nilus* commeth of none other caufe,
then that the windes *Etefiæ* so named, blowing
directly upon the ftreame thereof, hinder and
beate backe the waters from flowing into the
fea, which windes are commonly wont to arife,
and haue their feafon a long time after the increafe and rifing of *Nilus*: but imagine it were
otherwife, yet this of neceffitie muft follow, that
all riuers whatfoeuer hauing a full and direct
courfe againft the windes *Etefiæ*, fhall in like
maner fwell and grow ouer their bankes, and fo
much the rather, by how much the leffe and
weake the flouds themfelues are, whofe ftreames
are oppofed againft the fame. But there be
many rivers as well in *Syria* as in *Africa*, that
fuffer no fuch motion and change as hath bin
fayd

fayd of the floud *Nilus.* There is another opinion of leſſe credite and learning, albeit of
greater woonder and admiration then the firſt,
alleadging the cauſe of the riſing to be, for that
the riuer (ſay they) proceedeth from the Ocean
fea, which enuironeth the whole globe and circle
of the earth. The third opinion being more
caulme and modeſt then the reſt, is alſo more
falſe and unlikely then them both, affirming
that the increaſe and augmentation of *Nilus*
commes of the ſnowe waters molten and thawed
in thoſe regions, carying with it ſo much the
leſſe credit and authority, by how much the
more it is euident that the riuer comming from
Africa through the middeſt of *Æthiopia,* runnes
continually from the hotter countreys to the
colder, beeing in no wiſe probable, or any thing
likely that the waxing of the waters ſhould proceede of ſnowe. Many found proofes may be
brought to the weakening of this cauſe, whereby
we may geſſe how groſſely they erre whiche
thinke ſo greate a ſtreame to be increaſed by
ſnowe. What greater reaſon may be found to
the contrary, then that the windes blowing from
thoſe countreys are very warme by nature. Moreouer, the land it felfe is continually voyde of
rayne and yce, being moſt neceſſary that within
fiue dayes after the fall of ſnowe there ſhould
come

come rayne, where by it commeth to paſſe that
if it ſnowe in *Ægypt*, it muſt alſo of neceſſity Within fiue
rayne. The ſame is confirmed and eſtabliſhed dayes after
ſnowe, fal-
by the blackneſſe and ſwartneſſe of the people, leth rayne.
couloured by the vehement heate and ſcorching
of the ſunne : likewiſe by the ſwalowes and kytes
which continually keepe in thoſe coaſtes : laſtly
by the flight of the cranes toward the comming
of winter, which are always wont to flye out of
Scythia and the cold regions to theſe places,
where all the winter ſeaſon they make theyr
abode. Were it then that neuer ſo little ſnow
could fall in thoſe countreys by the which *Nilus*
hath his courſe, and from which he ſtretcheth
his head and beginning, it were not poſſible for
any of theſe things to happen which experience
prooueth to be true. They which talke of
Oceanus, grounding their iudgement vppon a
meere fable, want reaſon to prooue it. For I That there
is no ſea
thinke there is no ſuch ſea as the Ocean, but called
Ocean.
rather that *Homer* or ſome one of the auncient
Poets deuiſed the name, and made vſe thereof
afterwardes in their tales and poetry. Now if
it be expedient for me hauing refuted and dis-
alowed other mens iudgements, to ſet downe
mine owne. The reaſon why *Nilus* is ſo great
in ſommer I take to be this. In the winter- The true opinion of theſe
time the ſunne declining from his former race things.

vnder

vnder the colde winter ftarre, keepeth hys courfe
ouer the high countreys of *Africa*, and in thefe
fewe wordes is conteyned the whole caufe.   For
the funne the neerer he maketh his approch to
any region, the more he drinketh vp the moyfture thereof, and caufeth the riuers and brookes
of the fame countrey to runne very lowe.   But
to fpeake at large, and lay open the caufe in
more ample wyfe, thus the cafe ftandeth.   The
bringer to paffe and worker heereof is the funne,
beeing caryed ouer the hygh countreys of *Africa :*
For the fpring time with them beeyng very fayre
and cleare, the land hote, and the wyndes colde,
the funne paffing ouer them workes the fame
effecte as when it runneth in the middeft of

The caufe
why the
South and
Southweaft
wind bring
rayne. heauen in fommer, forfomuch as by vertue of
his beames gathering water vnto him, he caufeth
it to afcend into the fuperiour regions, where
the windes receiuing it, difpearfe the vapours
and refolue them againe, which is chiefely done
by the South and Southweft winde that blowe
from thefe countreys, beeing ftormy and full of
rayne.   Now the water drawne out of *Nilus* by
the funne, doth not in this fort fall downe
agayne in fhowres and drops of rayne, but is
quite fpent and confumed by the heate.   Toward the ende of winter, the funne drawing
towards the middeft of the fkye in like manner

as

as before, fucketh the water out of other riuers,
which is the caufe that being thus drawne vntill much rayne and fhowres increafe them
agayne, they become fleete and almoft drie.
Wherefore the riuer *Nilus*, into whome alone
no fhowres fall at any time, is for iuft caufe
loweft in winter, and higheft in fommer, forafmuch as in fommer the funne draweth moyfture
equally out of all riuers, but in winter out of
Nilus alone, this I take to be the caufe of the
diuers and changeable courfe of the riuer.
Heereof alfo I fuppofe to proceede the dryneffe
of the ayre in that region, at fuch time as the
funne deuideth his courfe equally, fo that in the
high countreys of *Africke* it is alwayes fommer :
whereas if it were poffible for the placing and
fituation of the heauens to be altered, that where
North is, there were South, and where South is,
North, the funne towardes the comming and
approach of winter departing from the middeft
of heauen, would haue his paffage in like fort
ouer *Europe,* as now it hath ouer *Africke,* and
worke the fame effects (as I iudge) in the riuer
Ifter, as now it doth in *Nilus.* In like maner, Ifter a great
the caufe why *Nilus* hath no mift or cloude riuer in
Europe.
arifing from it according as we fee in other
flouds, I deeme to be this, becaufe the countrey
is exceeding hote and parching, being altogether
vnfit

vnfit to fende vp any vapours, which vfually breathe and arife out of cold places. But let thefe things be as they are and haue bene alwayes.

The head and fountayne of *Nilus* where it is, or from whence it commeth, none of the *Ægyptians, Grœcians,* or *Africans* that euer I talked with, could tell me any thing, befides a certaine fcribe of *Mineruas* treafury in the city *Sais,* who feemed to me to fpeake merily, faying, that vndoubtedly he knewe the place, defcribing the fame in this manner. There be two mountaines (quoth he) arifing into fharpe and fpindled tops, fituate betweene *Syêne* a city of *Thebais,* and *Elephantina,* the one called *Crophi,* the other *Mophi.* From the vale betweene the two hilles doth iffue out the head of the riuer *Nilus,* being of an vnfearchable deapth, and without bottome, halfe of the water running towardes *Aegypt* and the North, the other halfe towardes *Æthiopia* and the South. Of the immeafurable deapth of the fountayne, the fcribe affirmed, that *Pfammetichus* King of the *Ægyptians* had taken triall, who founding the waters with a rope of many miles in length, was vnable to feele any ground or bottome: whofe tale (if any fuche thyng were done as he fayde) made me thinke, that in thofe places whereof

The fpring of the riuer Nilus vnfearchable.

The two mountaynes Crophi and Mophi.

whereof he fpake, were certayne gulfes or
whirlepooles very fwift, violente and raging,
whiche by reafon of the fall of the water from
the hilles, would not fuffer the line with the
founding leade to finke to the bottome, for
which caufe, they were fuppofed to be bottom-
leffe. Befides this, I coulde learne nothing of
any man. Neuertheleffe, trauelling to *Elephantina* to behold the thing with mine owne eyes,
and making diligent inquiry to knowe the truth,
I vnderftoode this, that takyng our iourney from
thence Southward to the countreys aboue, at
length we fhall come to a fteepe and bending
fhelfe, where the ryuer falleth with great violence, fo that we muft be forced to faften two
gables to each fide of the fhip, and in that fort
to hale and draw her forward, which if they
chaunce either to flip or breake, the veffell is by
and by driuen backwards by the intollerable rage
and violence of the waters. To this place from
the city *Elephantina* is four daies faile, where-
aboutes the riuer is ful of windings and turnings, like the floud *Meander,* and in length fo
continuing twelue fcheanes, all which way the
fhip of neceffity muft be drawne. After this,
we fhall arriue at a place very fmooth and
caulme, wherein is ftanding an Iland incompaffed rounde by the ryuer, by name *Tachampfo.*
The

The one halfe heereof is inhabited by the *Aegyptians,* the other halfe by the *Æthiopians,* whofe countrey is adioyning to the Southfide of the Ile. Not farre from the Iland is a poole of woonderfull and incredible bigneffe, about the which the Shepheards of *Æthiopia* haue their dwelling: whereinto, after we are declined out of the mayne ftreame, we fhall come to a riuer directly running into the poole, where going on fhore, we muft take our voyage on foote the fpace of forty dayes by the waters fide, the riuer *Nilus* it felfe beeyng very full of fharpe rockes and craggy ftones, by the which it is not pof-fible for a veffell to paffe. Hauing finifhed forty dayes iourney along the riuer, take fhipping againe, and paffe by water twelue dayes voyage, till fuch time as you arriue at a great city called *Meroe,* which is reputed for the chiefe and Metropolitane city of the countrey, the people whereof only of all the gods worfhip *Iupiter* and *Bacchus,* whome they reuerence with ex-ceeding zeale and deuotion. Likewise to *Iupiter* they haue planted an oracle, by whofe counfayle and voyce they rule their martiall affayres, making warre how oft foeuer, or againft whome-foeuer they are mooued by the fame. From this city *Meroe* by as many dayes trauell as yee take from *Elephantina* to the fame, you fhall come

The city Meroe.

come to a kind of people named *Automoly,*
which is to fay, traytours or runnagates, the
fame alfo in like manner being called *Afmach,*
which emporteth in the greeke tongue fuch as
ftande and attende at the Kings left hand.
Thefe men being whilome fouldyers in *Aegypt*
to the number of eyght thoufand and two
hundred, they reuolted from their owne coun- The foul-
treymen, and fled ouer to the *Æthiopians* for diers of
Ægypt for-
this occafion. Being in the time of King *Pfam-* fooke theyr
owne coun-
metichus difperfed and diuided into fundry garri- trey.
fons, fome at the city of *Elephantina,* and *Daphnæ
Pelufiæ,* againft the *Aethiopians,* other againft
the *Arabians* and *Syrians,* and thirdly at *Marea*
againft the *Africans* (in which places agreeably
to the order and inftitution of *Pfammetichus,* the
Perfian garrifons alfo did lie in munition) hauing
continued the fpace of three yeares in perpetuall
gard and defence of the lande, without fhift or
releafe, they fell to agreement amongft themfelues to leaue their King and countrey, and flye
into *Æthiopia:* which their intente *Pfammetichus* hearing, made after them incontinently,
and hauing ouertaken the army, humbly befought them with many teares, not to forfake
by fuche vnkind and vnnaturall wife their wiues,
children, and countrey gods, vnto whofe plaint
and intreaty, a rude royftrell in the company
fhewing

ſhewing his priuy members, made this aunfwere,
The tricke of a knaue.
whereſoeuer (quoth he) theſe be, there will I
finde both wyfe and children. After they were
come into *Aethiopia,* and had offered themſelues vnto the King of the ſoyle, they were by
him rewarded on this manner. Certayne of the
Aethiopians that were ſcarſely found harted to
the King, were depriued by him of all their
lands and poſſeſſions, which he franckly gaue
and beſtowed on the *Aegyptians.* By means of
theſe, the people of *Aethiopia* were brought
from a rude and barbarous kind of demeanour,
to farre more ciuill and manlike behauiour,
being inſtructed and taught in the maners and
cuſtomes of the *Aegyptians.* Thus the riuer
Nilus is founde ſtill to continue the ſpace of foure
monethes iourney by lande and water (leſſe then
in which time it is not poſſible for a man to
come from *Elephantina* to the *Automolians)*
A ſtory touching the ſpring of Nilus.
taking hys courſe and ſtreame from the Weſt
part of the world, and falling of the ſunne.

Howbeit in this place I purpoſe to recite a
ſtory told me by certayne of the *Cyrœneans,*
who fortuning to take a voyage to the oracle of
Ammon, came in talke with *Etearchus* King of
the *Ammonians,* where by courſe of ſpeache,
they fell at length to diſcourſe and common of
Nilus, the head whereof was vnſearchable, and
not

not to be knowne. In which place *Etearchus*
made mention of a certaine people called *Nama-
ſones* of the countrey of *Afrike*, inhabiting the
quickſands, and all the coaſt that lyeth to the
eaſt. Certayne of theſe men comming to the
court of *Etearchus*, and reporting dyuers ſtrange
and wonderfull things of the deſerts and wild
chaſes of *Africa*, they chaunced at length to tell
of certayne yong Gentlemen of theyr countrey,
iſſued of the chiefe and moſt noble families of A voyage
all their nation, who beeing at a reasonable age by certayne
very youthfull and valiant, determined in a young
brauery to go ſeeke ſtraunge aduentures, as well
other, as alſo this. Fiue of them being aſſigned
thereto by lot, put themſelues in voyage to go
ſearch and diſcry the wilderneſſe, and deſert
places of *Africa*, to the ende they might ſee
more, and make further report thereof then
euer any that had attempted the ſame. For
the ſea coaſt of Africa poynting to the North
pole, many nations do inhabite, beginning from
Aegypt, and continuing to the promontory
named *Soloes*, wherein *Africa* hath his end and
bound. All the places aboue the ſea are haunted
with wilde and ſauage beaſtes, beeing altogether
voyde and deſolate, peſtered with ſand, and exceeding drye. Theſe gentlemen-trauellers hauing made ſufficient prouiſion of water, and other

vyands

vyands neceſſary for theyr iourney, firſt of all
paſſed the countreys that were inhabited : and
next after that, came into the wylde and waſte
regions amongſt the caues and dennes of fierce
and vntamed beaſtes, through which they helde
on theyr way to the weſt parte of the earth.   In
which manner, after they had continued many
dayes iourney, and trauelled ouer a great part of
the ſandy countreys, they came at length to eſpy
certayne fayre and goodly trees, growing in a
freſh and pleaſaunt medowe, wherevnto incontinently making repayre, and taſting the fruite
that grewe thereon, they were ſuddenly ſur-
priſed and taken ſhort by a company of little
dwarfes, farre vnder the common pitch and
ſtature of men, whoſe tongue the gentlemen
knew not, neither was their ſpeache vnderſtoode
of them.   Being apprehended, they were lead
away ouer ſundry pooles and meares into a city,
where all the inhabitauntes were of the ſame
ſtature and degree with thoſe that had taken
them, and of colour ſwart and blacke.   Faſt
by the ſide of thys city ranne a ſwift and violent
riuer, flowing from the Weaſt to the Eaſt,
wherein were to be ſeene very hydeous and ter-
rible ſerpents called Crocodyles.   To this ende
drew the talke of *Etearchus* King of the *Ammo-*
nians, ſaue that he added beſides how the *Nama-*
ſonian

fonian gentlemen returned home to theyr owne
countrey (as the *Cyræneans* made recount) and
how the people alfo of the city whether they
were broughte, were all coniurers, and geuen
to the ftudy of the blacke arte. The floud that A City in-
had his paffage by the city, *Etearchus* fuppofed Necro-
to be the riuer *Nilus*, euen as alfo reafon it felfe mancers.
giueth it to be. For it floweth from *Africa*,
and hath a iuft and direct cut through the
middeft of the fame, following (as it fhould
feeme) a very like and femblable courfe vnto
the riuer *Ifter.*

Ifter beginning at the people of the *Celts*, and
the city *Pyrene* (the *Celts* keepe without the
pillers of *Hercules*, being neere neighbours to The defcrip-
the *Cynefians*, and the laft and vtmoft nation of riuer Ifter.
the wefterne people of *Europe*) deuideth *Europe*
in the middeft, and fcouring through the coaft,
it is helde by the *Iftryans* (people fo named and
comming of the *Milefians*) it laftly floweth into
the fea. Notwithftanding *Ifter* is well knowne
of many, for that it hath a perpetuall courfe
through countreys that are inhabited, but where
or in what parte of the earth *Nilus* hath his
fpring, no man can tell, forfomuch as *Africa*
from whence it commeth, is voyde, defert, and
vnfurnifhed of people, the ftreame and courfe
whereof, as farre as lyeth in the knowledge of
men,

men, we haue fet downe and declared, the end
of the riuer being in *Aegypt* where it breaketh
into the fea.

Aegypt is welny oppofite and directly fet
againft the mountaines of *Cilicia*, from whence
to *Synopis* ftanding in the *Euxine* fea, is fiue
daies iourney for a good footeman, by ftraight
and euen way.

The Ile *Synopis* lyeth iuft againft the riuer
Ifter, where it beareth into the fea, fo that *Nilus*
running through all the coaft of *Africa*, may in
fome manner be compared to the riuer *Ifter*,
howbeit, as touching the floud *Nilus* be it
hitherto fpoken.

Let us yet proceede to fpeake further of
Aegypt, both for that the countrey it felfe hath
more ftrange wonders then any nation in the
world, and alfo becaufe the people themfelues haue wrought fundry things more worthy
memory, then any other nation vnder the funne,
for which caufes, we thought meete to difcourfe
more at large of the region and people. The
Aegyptians therefore as in the temperature of
the ayre, and nature of the riuer, they diffent
from all other: euen fo in theyr lawes and
cuftomes they are vnlike and difagreeing from
all men.

In this countrey the women followe the
trade

Ægypt the moſt wonderfull nation in the world.

trade of merchandize in buying and felling : alfo The laws and cuſ- tomes of the people of Ægypt.
victualing and all kinde of fale and chapmandry,
whereas contrarywyfe the men remayne at home,
and play the good hufwives in fpinning and
weauing and fuch like duties.   In like manner,
the men carry their burthens on their heads, the
women on their fhoulders. Women make water
ftanding, and men crouching downe and cowring
to the ground.   They difcharge and vnburthen
theyr bellies of that which nature voydeth at
home, and eate their meate openly in the ftreetes
and high wayes, yeelding this reafon why they do
it, for that (fay they) fuch things as be vnfeemely
yet neceffary ought to be done in counfayle, but
and fuch as are decent and lawful, in the eyes
and viewe of all men. No woman is permitted to
do feruice or minifter to the gods or goddeffes,
that duty being proper and peculiar to men.
The fonne refufing to nourifh and fufteyne his
parents, hath no lawe to force and conftrayne The daughter bound to nouriſh her parents in need.
him to it, but the daughter be fhe neuer fo
vnwilling, is perforce drawne and compelled
thereto.   The priefts and minifters of the gods
in other countreys weare long hayre, and in
Aegypt are all rafed and fhaven.   Likewyfe
with other people it is an vfuall cuftome in for-
rowing for the dead to powle theyr lockes, and
efpecially fuch as are neareft touched with griefe,
but

C

but contrarywyfe the *Aegyptians* at the deceaffe
of their friends fuffer theyr hayre to growe,
beeing at other times accuftomed to powle and
cut it to the ftumps. Moreouer, the people of

The good
fellowfhip in
Ægypt
wher the
good man
and his hogs
dine to-
gether.
The vfe of
grayne is
very flender
in Aegypt.

all lands vfe to make difference betweene their
owne diet and the foode of beaftes, fauing in
Aegypt, where in barbarous and fwinifh maner
men and beafts feede ioyntly together. Befides
this, the people elfewhere haue their greateft
fuftenance by wheate, rye, and barly, which the
Aegyptians may not tafte of without great re-
proch and contumely, vfing neuerthelefle a kind
of wheate whereof they make very white and
fine bread, which of fome is thought to be
darnell or bearebarly. This at the firft hauing
mingled it with licour, they worke and mould
with their feete, kneading the fame afterwards
with their hands.

In this countrey alfo the manner is to circumcife and cut round about the fkinne from their
priuy parts, which none other vfe, except thofe
that haue taken letter, and learned the cuftome
from the *Aegyptians.* The men go in two garments, the women in one, ftitching to the infide of
the vefture a tape or caddefe to gird their apparell
clofe to them, which the people of other regions

The manner
of cafting of
account.

are wont to weare outwardly. The *Græcians* in
writing and cafting account, frame their letters,
and

and lay their counters from the left hand to the
right, the *Aegyptians* contrarywife proceede from
the right to the left, wherein alfo they frumpe
and gird at the *Græcians,* faying, that themfelues do all things to the right hand, which is
well and honeftly, but the *Grækes* to the left,
which is peruerfely and vntowardly. Furthermore, they vfe in writing two kind of charaćters
or letters, fome of the which they call holy and Their letters
or char-
diuine, other common and prophane. In the ećters.
feruice and worfhip of the gods, they are more
religious and deuout then any nation vnder
heauen. They drinke out of brafen pots, which
day by day they neuer fayle to cleanfe and wafh
very fayre and cleane, which manner and cuftome is not in a few of them, but in all. They
delight principally to go in frefh and cleane Cleanneffein
attyre with-
linnen, confuming no fmall part of the day in out pride.
wafhing their garmentes. They circumcife their
fecret partes for defire they haue to be voyde of
filth and corruption, efteeming it much better to
be accounted cleane, then comely. The priefts The cuftome
of the
and churchmen fhaue their bodies euery third priefts.
day, to the end that neyther lyce nor any kind
of vncleanneffe may take hold of thofe which
are dayly conuerfaunt in the honour and feruice
of the gods. The fame are arrayed in one
vefture of fingle linnen, and paper fhoes, without

out fufferance to go otherwife attired at any time. They purge and wafh themfelues euery day twice in the daye time, and as often in the night, vfing other ceremonies and cuftomes welny infinite that are not to be rehearfed. The felfe-fame priefts haue no fmall aduantage or com-modity in this, that they liue not of their owne, neither fpend or confume any thing of their priuate goodes and fubftaunce, but haue dayly miniftred and fupplied vnto them foode in great aboundance, as well the flefh of oxen as of

Their dyet. geefe. Their drinke is wine made of grapes, which in like maner is brought them in allow-ance. To take any kinde of fifhe, they hold it vnlawfull : and if by fortune they haue but feene or lightly behelde any beanes, they deeme themfelues the worfe for it a moneth after, forfomuch as that kind of pulfe is accounted vncleane. The reft alfo of the *Aegyptians* and common forte vfe very feldome or neuer to fowe beanes : and to eate the fame either rawe or fodden, they hold it a greeuous finne. The

The orders of prieft-hood. priefts take their orders in fuch wife, that euery one by turnes and courfes doth feruice to all the gods indifferently, no man being clarked or chofen to be the feuerall minifter of any one god alone. All thefe are gouerned by one generall prefident or Archbifhop. If any man

dye

dye, his fonne taketh the priefthoode in his ftead.
All neate and bullockes of the malekinde they
hold facred to *Epaphus,* whereof if they be in
minde to facrifice any, they fearche and trie hym
whether he be cleane or no after this manner.
If in all hys fkinne there appeare any one blacke
hayre, they by and by iudge him impure and
vnfit for facrifice, which triall is made by fome
of the priefts appoynted for the fame purpofe,
who taketh diligent view of the oxe both ftanding and lying, and turned euery way, that no
part may be vnfeene. After this, fearch is made
alfo of his mouth and tongue, whether all the
fignes and tokens appeare in him that fhould be
in a pure and vnfpotted beaft, of which fignes
we determine to fpeake in another booke. To
make fhort, he curioufly beholdeth the hayres of
his tayle whether they growe according to nature,
and be all white. If all thefe markes agree,
they tye a ribaund to one of his hornes, and
feare a marke on the other, and fo let him run,
and if any man aduenture to offer vp an oxe,
whofe hornes are not marked with the publike
feale or brandyron, he is by and by accufed by
the reft of his company, and condemned to dye.
Thefe are the meanes which they vfe in fearching and furueying theyr cattell, fuch as are to be
offered to the gods. Moreouer, in the time of

The manner
of trying
the bullocks
that are
facrificed
whether
they be
cleane or
otherwife.

facrifice

The order of facrificing. facrifice and oblation, this is their manner. The beaft that is fealed on the horne, being brought to the aultare and place of immolation, incontinent a fire is kindled, then fome one of the Chaplaynes taking a boule of wyne in his hands, drinketh ouer the oblation with his face towarde the temple, and calling with a loude voyce vpon the name of the god, giueth the beaft a wound and killeth him, The head of the beaft that is facrificed is accurfed. the head and hyde whereof, they beare into the market place, with many deteftable curffes, and diuelifh bannings, making fale thereof to the Merchaunts of *Greece.* Such of the *Aegyptians* as haue no place of fale or vfe of Merchaundife with the *Græcians,* caft both head and hyde into the riuer *Nilus.* In curffing the head of the flaine beaft they vfe this manner of imprecation, that if any euill or misfortune be to happen either to thofe which do the facrifice, or to the whole realme and dominion of *Aegypt,* it would pleafe the gods to turne all vpon that head. The like vfe and cuftome about the heads of fuch cattel as are killed in facrifice, and in time of offering for the prieft to drinke wine, is in all places alike throughout all the churches of *Aegypt,* in fo much, that it is growne into a fafhion in all the whole land, that no *Aegyptian* will tafte of the head of beaftes facrificed. Howbeit, there is choyfe and diuerfity of facri-

fice

fice with them, neyther is the same manner and
forme of oblation kept and obferued in euery
place. Now we will fhew and declare which
of all the goddeffes they chiefly honour, and
in whofe name they folemnize and celebrate
the greateft feaft. Hauing therefore moft de-
uoutely fpent the eue or day before the feaft in
folemne fafting and prayer, they facrifice an
Oxe, whofe hyde incontinently they pull off and
take out his entrayles, fuffering the leafe and fat
to remayne within him. After that, they hewe
off the fhanke bones, with the lower part of the
loyne and fhoulders, likewife the head and the
necke, which done, they farce and ftuffe the
body with halowed bread, hony, rayfons, figges,
franckincenfe, myrrhe, and other precious odours.
Thefe things accomplifhed they offer him vp in
facrifice, pouring into him much wine and oyle,
and abiding ftill fafting, vntill fuch time as the
offering be finifhed. In the meane fpace while
the facrifice is burning, they beate and torment
themfelues with many ftripes, whereby to fatisfy
and appeafe the wrath and difpleafure of the
gods. Hauing left off on this manner to afflict
and crucifie their flefh, the refidue of the facrifice is fet before them, wherewith they feaft and
refrefhe their hunger. It is a cuftome receyued
throughout all the region, to offer bullocks and
calues

calues of the malekinde, if in cafe they be found
immaculate and pure, according to the forme

of their lawe : howbeit, from kine and heiffers,
they abfteyne moft religioufly, accounting them
as holy and confecrate to the goddeffe *Ifis*, whofe
image is carued and framed like a woman, with
a paire of hornes on hir head, like as the *Græcians* defcribe and fet foorth *Iö*. Hereof it proceedeth that the people of *Aegypt* do moft of
all other beaftes worfhip and reuerence a cowe,
for which caufe, none of that nation neither
men nor women will eyther kiffe a *Græcian*, or
fo much as vfe hys knife to cut any thing, his
fpit to roft, his pot to boyle, or any other thing
belonging to them, difdayning and loathing the
very meate that hath bin cut with a *Græcians*
knife, forfomuch as in *Greece* they feede of all
neate indifferently both male and feamale. If
an oxe or cowe chaunce to die, they bury them

on this wife, the kine and females they caft into
the riuer, burying the oxen in fome of the
fuburbes with one of his hornes fticking out of
the ground for a token, lying on this maner
vntill they be rotten. At an ordinary and appoynted time, there ariueth a fhip from the Ile
Profopitis fituate in that part of *Aegypt* which
is named *Delta*, being in compaffe nine fcheanes,
which is 63 miles. In this Iland are planted
many

many cities, one of the which continually fur-
nifheth and fends foorth the aforefaid fhip,
hauing to name *Atarbechis*, wherein ftandeth a
faire and goodly temple dedicated to *Venus*.
From this city *Atarbechis*, many people are
woont to ftray and wander into other townes of
Aegypt. The fhip comming to land at euery
city, takes vp the bones of the dead oxen, and
caries them all to one place where they are
buryed together. The law alfo commaundeth
the felfe fame manner to be kept and obferued
in the fepulture and burying of other cattell that
dye in the land, from the flaughter of the which
generally the *Aegyptians* abfteyne. Neuerthelefec,
fuch as abiding in the prouince of *Thebes* in the
temple of *Iupiter Thebanus*, are inuefted with the
orders of priefthoode, vfe the fame abftinence from
fheepe, and flayne goates vpon the aultars of the
gods, for in *Aegypt* the fame gods haue not the
fame kinde of diuine honour in euery place and
with euery people, fauing *Ifis* and *Ofyris*, the
one a goddeffe, the other a god, which are of all
men worfhipped alyke. This *Ofyris* is of the
Aegyptians thought to be *Bacchus*, albeit for
fome refpect they name him otherwife. Contrary to thefe, fuch as are belonging to the pallace of *Mendes*, and are conteyned within the
precinct and limits of that fheere, withholde
themfelues

The caufe why fome of the Ægyptians will kill no fheepe.

themfelues from goates, and make facrifice of fheepe. The *Thebanes* therefore, and fuch as following their example efchew and auoyde the flaughter and killing of fheepe, teftifie themfelues to be mooued heerevnto by a law, becaufe that *Iupiter* on a time refufing to be feene of *Hercules* who greately defired to behold him, at his inftant prayers cut off the head of a ramme, and ftripping off the fell, caft it ouer him, and in fuch manner fhewed himfelfe to his fonne, whereof the *Aegyptians* framing the image of *Iupiter*, made him to haue a rammes head, of whome, the *Ammonians* tooke that cuftome, whych are an ofspring and braunch growne from two fundry nations the *Aegyptians* and *Aethiopians*, as well may be feene by their language which is a medley of both tongues: who feeme

Whence the Ammonians drew theyr name.

for this caufe to haue named themfelues *Ammonians*, for that they hold the oracle of *Iupiter* whome the *Aegyptians* call by the name of *Ammon*. In this refpecte the *Thebanes* abfteyne from the bloud of rammes and fheepe, efteeming them as holy and diuine creatures. Howbeit, one day in the yeare which they keepe feftiuall to *Iupiter* they kill a ramme, and taking off the fkynne, they couer therewith the image, wherevnto incontinent they bring the picture of *Hercules*, after which, they beate the naked flefh of the

the ramme for a good feafon. The facrifice
being in this fort accomplifhed, they bury the
body in a religious and halowed veffel. This
Hercules they recken in the number of the
twelue gods, as for the other *Hercules* of whome
the *Græcians* make mention, the *Aegyptians* are
altogether vnacquainted with him, neyther do
they feeme at any time to haue heard of him.
This name I fuppofe to haue come firft from
Aegypt into *Græce*, and to haue bene borrowed The name
of Hercules
of them, howfoeuer the *Græcians* diffemble the taken from
matter, to make the inuention feeme their owne : the Ægyp-
tians.
wherevpon I grounde wyth greater confidence,
for that the parents of *Hercules, Amphytrio* and
Alcmæna are by countrey and lynage *Aegyptians.*
Likewife in *Aegypt,* the name of *Neptune,* and
the gods called *Diofcuri,* was very ftraunge, and
vnheard of, neyther would they be brought by
any meanes to repute them in the fellowfhip
and company of the gods. And if in cafe they
had taken the name of any god from the *Græcians,* it is very credible that as well as of the
reft, nay aboue the reft, they would haue made
chofe of *Neptune* and the other, were it that at
thofe dayes trade of merchandife, and voyaging
by fea were vfed eyther by them into *Græce,* or
by the *Græcians* into *Aegypt,* which I fuppofe
and thinke to haue bene. It is therefore moft
founding

founding and agreeable to truth, that if anything had bene borrowed by them, the name
of *Neptune* rather then *Hercules* had crept
into their manners and religion. Befides this,
the godhead and name alfo of *Hercules* is of
greate continuance and antiquity in *Aegypt*, infomuch that (by their faying) 17000 yeares are
paffed, fince the raigne of King *Amafis* in tyme
of whofe gouernaunce, the number of the gods
was increafed from eight to twelue, whereof
Hercules was then one. Heerein not contented
with a flippery knowledge, but mooued with
defire to learne the truth, I came in queftion
with many aboute the fame caufe, and tooke
fhipping alfo to *Tyrus* a city of *Phœnicia*, where
I had heard fay that the temple of *Hercules* was
founded. Being landed at *Tyrus*, I beheld the
pallace beautified and adorned with gifts of
ineftimable price, and amongft thefe, two croffes,
one of tried and molten gold, another framed of
the precious gemme *Smaragdus*, whiche in the
night feafon fent foorth very bright and fhining
beames, forthwith falling into parle with the
chaplaines and priefts of the temple, I demaunded them during what fpace the chappell
had ftoode, and how long fince it was built,
whofe talke and difcourfe in nothing agreed with
the *Græcians* affirming, that the temple tooke his
beginning

beginning with the city, from the firſt foundation and groundley whereof, two thouſand and
three hundred yeares are expired. I ſaw alſo
in *Tyrus* another temple vowed to *Hercules*
ſurnamed *Theſius.* In like ſort, I made a iorney
to *Thaſus*, where I light vpon a chappell erected
by the *Phœnicians*, who enterpriſing a voyage
by ſea to the knowledge and diſcouery of *Europe*,
built and founded *Thaſus*, fiue mens ages before
the name of *Hercules* was knowne in *Greece.*
Theſe teſtimonies do plainely prooue that *Hercules* is an auncient god and of long durance.
For whiche cauſe amongſt all the people of
Greece they ſeeme to haue taken the beſt courſe,
that honour *Hercules* by two ſundry temples, The two temples of Hercules in Greece.
to one they ſhew reuerence as to an immortall
god, whome they call *Hercules Olympius*, to
another, as to a chiefe peere, and moſt excellente
perſon amongſt men. Many other things are
noyſed by the *Grœcians*, albeit very raſhly and
of ſlender ground : whoſe fond and vndiſcret tale
it is, that *Hercules* comming into *Aegypt*, was
taken by the *Aegyptians*, and crowned with a
garland, who were in full mind to haue made
him a ſacrifice to *Iupiter.* Unto whoſe aultare
being lead with greate pompe and celerity, he
remayned very meeke and tractable, vntill ſuch
time as the prieſt made an offer to ſlay him, at
what

what time recalling his fpirits, and laying about him with manfull courage, he made a great flaughter of all fuch as were prefent and ftroue againft him. By which theyr fabulous and incredible narration they flatly argue, how ignoraunt and vnaquaynted they be with the maners of *Aegypt*, for vnto whome it is not lawfull to make oblation of any brute beaft, but of fwine, oxen, calues and geefe : coulde they fo farre ftray from duty and feare of the gods, as to ftayne and blemifh their aultars with the bloud of men : Agayne, *Hercules* being alone in the hands of fo many *Aegyptians*, can it ftande wyth any credence or lykelyhoode, that of hymfelfe he fhould be able to flay fo greate a multitude : But let vs leaue thefe fables, and proceede forwarde to the truth. Such therefore of thys people as flye the bloudfhead and flaughter of goates (namely the *Mendefians*) lay for theyr ground, that *Pan* was in the number of the eyght gods which were of greater ftanding and antiquitie then the twelue.

The reafon why in fome partes of Ægypt they will kill no goates.

The forme and image of the god *Pan*, both the paynters and caruers in *Aegypt* frame to the fame fimilitude and refemblance as the *Grœcians* haue expreffed and fet him foorth by, making him to haue the head and fhankes of a goate, not that they thinke him to be fo, but rather like the other gods. Notwithftanding the caufe whereby

whereby they are mooued to portray and fhadow
him in fuch fort, is no greate and handfome tale
to tell, and therfore we are willing to omit it by
filence, fufficeth it that we knowe how as well
bucke as dooe goates are no pety faincts in this
countrey, in fomuch that with the *Mendefians*
goateheards are exalted aboue the common forte,
and much more fet by then any other degree of
men, of which company, fome one is alwayes of
chiefe eftimation, at whofe death, all the quarter
of *Mendefia* is in great forrow and heauines,
whereof it commeth, that as well the god *Pan*
himfelfe, as euery male-goate is called in the
Ægyptian fpeach *Mendes*. In thefe parts of
Ægypt it hapned that a goate of the malekinde
in open fight clofed with a woman, whiche be- A Goate
came very famous and memorable throughout a woman.
all the countrey. An hogge is accounted with beafts wurft
them an vncleane and defiled beaft, which of.
if any paffing by fortune to touch, his next Hogheards
worke is to go wafhe and dowfe himfelfe clothes account.
and all in the riuer, for which caufe, of all their
proper and natiue countreymen, only fuch as
keepe fwine, are forbidden to do worfhip in the
temples. No man will vouchfafe to wed his
daughter to a fwineheard, nor take in marriage
any of their difcent and iffue feamale, but they
mutually take and yeeld their daughters in marriage

riage betweene themfelues. Of the number of
the gods onely *Liber* and the Moone are facrificed vnto with hogges, whereof making oblation at the full of the moone, for that fpace alfo
they feede of porke and hogs flefh. The reafon
why the people of *Ægypt* kill fwyne at this
time, and at all other times boyle in so great
defpight and hatred againft them, bycaufe
mine eares glowed to heare it, I thought it
maners to conceale it. Swyne are offered

Divine facri-
fice to Liber
and Luna. vp to the Moone in this manner : the hogge
ftanding before the aultare, is firft flayne, then
taking the tip of hys tayle, the milt, the
call, and the fewet, they lay them all together,
fpreading ouer them the leafe or fat that lyeth
about the belly of the fwine, which immediately
they caufe to burne in a bright flame. The
flefh remayning they eate at the full of the
moone, which is the fame day whereon the facrifice is made, abhorring at all other times the flefh
of fwine as the body of a ferpent. Such as be
of poore eftate, and flender fubftaunce, make the
picture and image of a hogge in paaft or dowe,
whiche beeing confequently boyled in a veffell,
they make dedication thereof to their gods.
Another feaft alfo they keepe folemne to *Bacchus*,
in the which towarde fupper they fticke a fywne
before the threfhold or entry of their dwelling
places,

places, after which, they make reſtitution thereof to the ſwinehearde agayne of whom they
bought it. In all other pointes pertayning to
thys feaſt, ſo like the *Græcians* as may be,
ſauing that they ſquare a little, and vary heerein.
For the manner of *Greece* is in this banquet to
weare about their neckes the ſimilitude that
the Latins name *Phallum*, wrought and carued
of figtree, in ſtead whereof, the *Ægyptians* haue
deuiſed ſmall images of two cubites long, whiche
by meanes of certayne ſtrings and coardes they
cauſe to mooue and ſtirre as if they had ſence
and were liuing. The cariage of theſe pictures
is committed to certayne women that beare
them too and fro through the ſtreetes, making
the part of the image (which is as bigge as
all the bodye beſides) to daunce and play in
abhominable wiſe. Faſt before theſe marcheth
a piper, at whoſe heeles the women followe
incontinent with ſundry pſalmes and ſonets to
the god *Bacchus*. For what cauſe that one
member of the picture is made too big for the
proportion and frame of the body, and alſo
why, that, only of all the body is made to
mooue, as they refuſed to tell for religion, ſo
we deſired not to heare for modeſty. Howbeit,
Melampus ſonne of *Amytheon* was falſly ſup-
poſed to haue bin ignoraunt in the ceremonies
of

Superſtition
oft times
runneth into
moſt filthy
deuiſes.

D *

Melampus the firſt founder of this ceremonie in Greece. In the time of Herodotus the name of Philoſophers was ſtraunge.

of *Ægypt*, in the whiche he was very ſkilfull and cunning. By whom the *Greekes* were firſt inſtructed in the due order and celebration of *Bacchus* feaſt (whome they worſhipped by the name of *Dionyſius*) and in many other ceremonies and religious obſervations pertayning to the ſame. Notwithſtanding ſomething wanted in this deſcription, which was after added, and in more perfect and abſolute manner ſet downe by certayne graue and wiſe men called Philoſophers, which liued in the ſecond age after him. Moſt euident it is that the picture of *Phallum* worne of the *Græcians* in the feaſt of *Bacchus*, was found out and deuiſed by him, whoſe diſcipline in this point the *Græcians* obſerve at this day. This *Melampus* was a man of rare wiſedome, well ſeene in the art of diuination and ſouthſaying, the author and firſt founder to the *Græcians* as well of other things which he had learned in *Ægypt*, as alſo of ſuch ſtatutes and obſeruances as belong to the feaſt of *Dionyſius*, only a few things altered which he thought to amend. For why, to thinke that the *Græcians* and *Ægyptians* fell into the ſame forme of diuine worſhip by hap hazard or plaine chaunce, it might ſeeme a very hard and vnreaſonable geſſe, ſithence it is manifeſt that the *Greekes* both vſe the ſelfe-

ſame

fame cuftome, and more then that, they kept
it of olde. Much leffe can I be brought to
fay, that either this fafhion or any other hath
bene tranflated and deriued from *Greece* into
Ægypt. I rather iudge that *Melampus* comming from *Phœnicia* into *Beotia,* accompanyed
with *Cadmus* and fome other of the *Tyrians,*
was by them made acquaynted with all fuch
rites and ceremonies as in the honour of *Dionyfius* are vfed by the *Greekes.* True it is,
that the names by which the gods are vfually
called, are borrowed and drawne from the
Ægyptians, for hearing them to be taken from
the *Barbarians* as the chiefe inuenters and
deuifers of the fame, I haue found not only that
to be true, but alfo that for the moft parte
they are brought out of *Ægypt.* For fetting
afide *Neptune* and the gods called *Diofcuri*
(as before is declared) *Iuno, Venus, Themis,*
the Graces, the Nymphes *Nereides,* all the
names of the gods and goddeffes haue bene
euermore knowne and vfurped in *Ægypt.* I
fpeake no more then the *Ægyptians* teftify,
which auouch fincerely that neyther *Neptune*
nor the gods *Diofcuri* were euer heard of in
their land. Thefe names I iudge to haue
bene deuifed by the *Pelafgians,* except *Neptune,*
whofe name I fuppofe to be taken from the
people

people of *Africa,* forfomuch as from the beginning no nation on the earth but only the
Africanes vfed that name, amongft whome,
Neptune hath alwayes bene reuerenced with
celeftiall and diuine honours, whome the *Ægyptians* alfo denie not to be, albeit they fhewe and
exhibite no kinde of diuine honour towardes
him. Thefe and fuche like cuftomes (which
we purpofe to declare) haue the *Greekes* borrowed of the *Ægyptians:* neuerthelefle, the
image of *Mercury* I rather deeme to haue
proceeded from the maners of the *Pelafgians,*
then from the vfuall and accuftomed wont of
Ægypt, and principally to haue growne in vfe
wyth the *Athenians,* whofe fact confequently
became a paterne and example to the reft of the
Græcians. For the felfefame foyle was ioyntly
held and inhabited both of the *Athenians* (which
were of the right lignage of *Hellen*) and likewife of the *Pelafgians,* who for the fame caufe
began to be reckoned for *Græcians.* Which
things are nothing maruaylous to thofe that are
fkilfull and acquaynted with the worfhip and
religion whych the *Græcians* yeeld to the three
fonnes of *Vulcane* named *Cabiri,* which diuine
ceremonies are now frefh in *Samothracia,* and
were taken and receyued from the *Pelafgians.*
The caufe is, that thofe *Pelafgians* whome we
said

Cabiri the three fonnes of Vulcane.

faid before to haue had all one territorie with the *Athenians*, dwelt fometime alfo in *Samo-thracia*, by whome the people of that foyle were taught and indoctrined in the ceremonies appertinent to *Bacchus*. Firſt therefore the people of *Athens* following the ſteps of the *Pelafgians*, caufed the picture of *Mercury* to be carued in fuche forte as we haue heard. For authority and proofe why the image ſhould be thus framed, the men of *Pelafgos* recited a myſterie out of holy bookes, which is yet kept and conferued in the religious monuments of *Samo-thracia*. The felfefame in prayer and inuocation to the heauenlye powers, made oblation of all creatures indifferentlye, and wythout refpect (whyche I came to knowe at *Dodona*) geuing no names at all to the gods, as beeyng flatly ignoraunte howe to call them. Generally they named them Θεοί, gods, in that θέντες εἴχον κόσμω, that is, they difpofed and placed in order all the countreyes and regions on earth. In tract of tyme, the names and appellations of the powers diuine vfed in *Ægypt*, grew alfo in knowledge with the *Greekes*: enfuing which, the name alfo of *Dionyfius*, otherwife called *Bacchus*, came to light, albeit, long after that time and in later dayes. A fmall time exfpired, the *Greekes* counfayled with the oracle in *Dodona* to the fame

Dodona fomtime the chiefe oracle in Greece. fame ende and purpofe. This chayre of prophecy was in thofe dayes the only and moſt auncient feate in the land of *Greece*, whether the *Pelafgians* repayring, demaunded the oracle if the furnames of the gods receiued and taken from the *Barbarians*, might be lawfully frequented in *Greece:* whereto aunfwere was geuen, that they fhoulde be reteined : for whyche caufe, yeelding facrifice to the gods, fuch names were

The beginning of the pagans gods. helde by the men of *Pelafgos*, and laſtly obferued of the *Grœcians*. Howbeit, what original or beginning the gods had, or whether they were euermore time out of mind : finally, what forme, figure, or likeneſſe they bare, it was neuer fully and perfectly knowne till of late dayes. For *Hefiodus* and *Homer* (which were not paſſing 400 yeares before us) were the firſt that euer made the gods to be borne and fproong of certaine progenies like vnto men, aſſigning to euery one a byname, proper and peculiar honours, fundry crafts and fciences wherein they excelled, not leauing fo much as the fauour and portraytour of any of the gods fecrete and vndefcried. As for fuche poets as are faide to haue gone before thefe, they feeme to me to haue liued after them. The firſt of thefe things (I meane the names of the natures celeſtiall) to haue bene planted in *Greece* in fuch forte as hath bene declared,

declared, the priefts at *Dodona* do iuftly wit-
neffe. Now for this of *Hefiode* and *Homer* to
be no otherwyfe then is faid, I pawne mine owne
credit. Furthermore, of the oracles in *Africke*
and *Greece* the *Ægyptians* blafe this rumor, and
principally fuch as are employed in the feruice
and minifterie of *Iupiter Thebanus :* by whome
it is fayde, that certaine men of the *Phœnicians*
comming to *Thebes*, ftale priuily from thence
two women accuftomed to minifter in the
temple of *Iupiter*, one of the which they fold in
Lybia, the other in *Greece*, by whofe meanes
and aduife it came to paffe, that in each countrey the people created an oracle. Heereat
ꙇ fomewhat abafhed, and requefting earneftly how
and in what manner they came to knowe this,
they made me aunfwere, that leauing no corner
vnfearched whereby to come to knowledge of
their women, and not able to finde how they
were beftowed, newes was brought at length of
their plight and condition. Thus farre was I
certified by the *Thebane* prelates, wherevnto I
deeme it conuenient to adde fuch things as were
notified vnto mee at *Dodona* by the priefts there,
who vndoubtedly affyrme how in times forepaft
and long ago, two blacke pigeons tooke theyr
flight from the countrey of *Thebes* in *Ægypt*,
fcouring with fwift courfe through the fky, one

The begin-
ning of the
oracles in
Africke and
Greece.

A tale of
two pigeons.

of

of the which fortuned to light in *Africa*, the
other in that part of *Greece* where *Dodona* is
now fituate, where pointing vpon a mighty tall
beech, fhe was heard to fpeake in a voice humane,
like vnto a man, warning the people to erect an
oracle or feate of diuination in that place, being
fo thought good, and prouided by the deftinies.
Whiche admonition the people taking (as well
they might) to come by the inftinct and motion
of the gods, did as they were commaunded by the
doue.   In like manner it fell out that in *Lybia*
the people were ftirred vp and incenfed by the
other doue to the planting and erection of a feate
propheticall, named the oracle of *Ammon*, being
alfo confecrate to the name of *Iupiter*. Thefe
things we receiued of the credite and authoritie
of the *Dodoneans*, confirmed and eftablifhed by
the generall confente of thofe that had the care
and charge of the temple. Of thefe women
priefts refident in the temple of *Dodona*, the
eldeft and moft auncient had to name *Promenca*,
the fecond *Timareta*, the third and yongeft
Nicandra. Neuerthelelffe of thefe matters fuch
is my iudgement. If any fuch religious and
holy women were by ftealth of the *Phenicians*
tranfported and caryed away into *Lybia* and
Greece, I coniecture that the one of thefe was
fold at *Thefprotus*, in that parte of the region
which

which earſt was in the poſſeſſion of the *Pelaſ-
gians*, and is at this preſent reputed for a portion
of *Hettus :* where, hauing ſcrued certayne yeares,
in proceſſe of time ſhe brought in vſe the diuine
ceremonies of *Iupiter*, vnder ſome beach tree
growing in thoſe coaſtes. For what could be
more likely or conueniente, then for her to
eſtabliſh ſome monument in the ſacred honour
of *Iupiter*, in whoſe ſeruice and religion ſhe had
bene long time conuerſaunt at *Thebes* in *Ægypt.*
Which her ordinance at length grewe into the
cuſtome of an oracle. The ſame beeing perfect
alſo in the Greeke language, diſcouered vnto
them in what ſort the *Phenicians* had likewiſe
made ſale of hir ſiſter to the people of *Africa*.
The ſacred and deuoute women of *Dodona*
reſyaunt in the pallace of the great god *Iupiter*,
ſeeme for none other cauſe to haue called theſe
Ægyptian puſils two doues, then for that they
were come from barbarous countreys, whoſe
tongue and manner of pronouncing ſeemed to
the *Græcians* to founde like the voyce of birds.
And whereas they ſhewe that in time the doue
began to vtter playne language, and ſpeake like
men, naught elſe is meant heereby then that
ſhe vſed ſuch ſpeech as they knew and vnder-
ſtood, being ſo long eſteemed to emulate and
follow the noyſe of birds as ſhe remained in her
barbarous

barbarous kind of fpeach and pronuntiation.
For how is it credible that a pigeon in deede
could haue vfurped the voice and vtteraunce
of a man: and alleadging yet further that it
was a blacke doue, they argued her more
playnely to haue bene a woman of *Ægypt*, the
flower of whofe beauty is a fayre browne blew,
tanned and burnt by the fyery beames of the
funne.   Agayne, the oracles themfelues, that of
Thebes, and this of *Dodona*, are welnye in all
poyntes agreeable.   To fpeake nothing of the
maner and order of fouthfaying in the temples
of *Greece*, whych any man with halfe an eye
may eafily difcerne to haue bene taken from
Ægypt.   Let it ftand alfo for an euident and
Inuentions   vndoubted verity, that affemblies at feftiuals,
of the
Ægyptians.   pompes and pageants in diuine honour, talke
and communication with the gods by a media-
tour or interpretour, were inuented in *Ægypt*,
and confequently vfed in *Greece*.   Which I
thinke the rather, for that the one is old and of
long continuance, the other frefhe and lately
The feaftes   put in practife.   It is not once in a yeare that
of Diana,
I fis, and   the *Ægyptians* vfe thefe folemne and religious
Minerua.   meetings, but at fundry times and in fundry
places, howbeit, chiefly and with the greateft
zeale and deuotion at the city *Bubaftis*, in the
honour of *Diana*.   Next after that at *Bufiris*, in
the

the celebration of *Iſis* feaſt, where alſo ſtandeth
the moſt excellent and famous temple of
Iſis, who in the Greeke tongue is called
Δήμητηρ, which is to wit, *Ceres.* Thirdly, an The feaſt of the Sunne.
aſſembly is held in the city *Sais* in the prayſe
and reuerence of *Minerua.* Fourthly, at *Heliopolis* in honour of the ſunne. Fiftly, at *Butis*
in remembraunce of *Latona.* In the ſixt and
laſt place at the city *Papremis,* to the dignity The celebra-
and renowne of *Mars.* Moreouer, ſuch of this nas feaſt
people as with entyre and affectionate zeale and Mars.
moſt religiouſly obſerue the feaſt at *Bulaſtis,*
behaue and beare themſelues on this maner.
Certayne ſhippes being addreſſed, wherein infinite numbers of men and women ſayle towards
the city, in the meane feaſon whiles they be in
voiage on the water, certaine of the women play The maner
vpon drums and tabers, making a great ſound repaire to
and noyſe, the men on pipes. Such as want of Diana.
theſe implements, clap their hands and ſtraine
their voice in ſinging to the higheſt degree. At
what city ſoeuer they ariue, happely ſome of the
women continue their mirth and diſport on the
timbrels, ſome other raile, reuile and ſcold at the
dames of the city beyond meaſure : many trauiſe
and daunce minionly : other caſt vp their clothes,
and openly diſcouer and bewray their ſhame,
doing this in all thoſe cities that are neere adioyning

ioyning to the riuers fide. Being affembled and
gathered together at *Bubaftis,* they honour the
feaft day with principall folemnity, making large
offrings to *Diana,* wherein is greater expence
and effufion of grape wine then all the yeare befides. To this place by the voice of the countrey
are wont to repayre 7000 men and women,
befides children, and thus they paffe the time at
Bubaftis. Now in what maner they folemnize
the facred day of *Ifis* at the city *Bufiris,* we declared before, wherein their vfage is after the
due performance and accomplifhment of the
facrifice, to whip and fcourge themfelues in
lamentable wife, and that not one or two, but
many thoufandes of eache degree both men
and women : neuerthelefie, by what meanes, or
wherewithal they beate and vexe their bodies in
this fort, I may not difclofe. Howbeit fuch of
the people of *Caria* as foiourne and make their
abode in *Ægypt,* ftricken with a deeper remorfe
of finne, in this point of zeale and ardency go beyond the *Ægyptians,* in that they hackle and flice
their foreheads with kniues and daggers : whereby it is plainely geuen vs to vnderftande that
they come of forreine nations, and not of the
homeborne and naturall people of the land. In
like manner meeting (as before) at the city
Sais, there to accomplifhe the rites and ceremonies

monies due to the day, at the approche and
neere poynt of the evening, they furnifh and
befet their houfes with torches and lampes, The feaft of
lampes.
which being replenifhed with pure oyle mingled
with falte, they giue fire to the weike, and
fuffer them to continue burning till the next
morning, naming the day by the feaft of lampes.
Such as refort not to this feaft, do neuerthelefle
at their owne homes giue due honour to the
night, placing in euery corner of theyr houfe an
" infinite number of tapers and candles, the cuftome being not only kept at *Sais*, but fpread
and fcattered throughout the whole region. But
for what ende this night is helde folemne by
lighting of lampes, a certayne myfticall and
religious reafon is yeelded which we muft keepe
fecret. At *Heliopolis* and *Butis* onely, facrifice,
without execution of any other ceremonies, is
done to the gods. Likewife at *Papremis* they
retayne the fame cuftome of diuine feruice and
worfhipping as in other places. At the funne
going downe, certayne chofen men of the
priefts, being few in number, and ferioufly held A combate
of priefts.
and bufied about the image, the moft parte
ftanding before the dore of the temple armed
with clubs as much as they can weilde : ouer
againft whome on the contrary fide, other,
more then a thoufand men (of the number of
thofe

thofe that come to worfhip) all ftrongly furnifhed
and prepared with bats in their handes. The
day before the feaft, the picture or image framed
of wood, is by meanes of a few (affigned to the
miniftery and care of the woodden god) conueyed
out of a fmall temple make of light timber gor-
geoufly gilded : into another facred and religious
houfe, being thither drawne by the minifters
themfelues vppon a wayne of foure wheeles,
whereon the temple itfelfe is placed, and the
image alfo conteined therein. Drawing neere
to the temple with their cariage, the clubbes
ftanding before the dore wyth threates and cruell
manaces forbid them to enter : incontinent the
band of men ouer againft them coming with might
and maine to affift the image, and encountring
with thofe that kept the temple, lay on fuche
rude blowes, that hardly anye efcapeth without
hys crowne crackt in manye places. Wherein alfo
I fuppofe that many men mifcarry and came
fhort home, albeit they flatly denie that of a
wound fo taken any man euer perifhed. The
homelings and peculiar people of that countrey
alleadge this reafon of the battell. In this
temple (faye they) did fometimes inhabite the
mother of the god *Mars*, who feeking at the
eftate of ripe yeares againft the lawe of nature
to haue fociety with his owne mother, tooke the
repulfe,

The caufe
of this com-
bate.

repulfe, and was reiected by her minifters that
knew him not, whereat the god ftorming in
great rage, purchafed ayde out of the cities ad-
ioynaunt, and made way perforce, to the greate
difcomfiture and dammage of thofe as fought to
refift him, for which caufe, they yet folemnize
to *Mars* a feaft of broken pates and brufed cof- The feaft of
tards, enacting moreouer by the vertue of their pates.
religion, that no man fhould haue carnall copu-
lation with a woman in the temple, neyther attempt to fet his foote within the dores of any
fuche houfe of religion, vnleffe after the flefhly
knowledge of women he firft wafh and cleanfe
his body wyth pure water, whiche cuftome onely
taketh place amongft the *Græcians* and *Ægyp-*
tians, beeing the vfe in other nations to accompany with their women in the churches and
palaces of their gods, and alfo prefently after
fuch fecret actes, without any regard of puri-
fying themfelves, to rufh into the houfes of diuine
honour, making no difference betweene men and
other brutifh and vnreafonable creatures. For
it is feene (fay they) how other things that haue A reafon
drawn from
life and fence, meddle themfelues each with the vfe of
beaftes to
other euen in fuch places as the gods were wor- defend the
maners of
fhipped, which if it were a thing fo odious and men.
difpleafaunt in the eyes of the higher powers, no
doubt the beaftes themfelues would efchue and
auoyde

auoyde it, whofe doings together with their
iudgement I flatly difalow. Howbeit, vnderftand we, that as well in thefe things whereof
we haue intreated, as in all other the *Ægyptians*
are led with a fingular fuperftition. *Ægypt* alfo
it felfe albeit it abutte and poynt vpon the
countrey of *Lylia*, yet is it not ouermuch pef-
tered with beaftes. Such as the lande bringeth
vp and foftereth, are reputed holy, and by no
meanes to be violated or harmed by any, fome
of which haue their nouriture and foode together
with the people of the foyle : otherfome are more
wilde, fierce, and intractable, refufing fo gently
to come to hand. The caufe of thefe things, why
creatures vnreafonable are fo highly honoured
of this people, I may not without breach of
piety reveale : which things of fet purpofe I
haue endeauoured to conceale and keepe fecrete,
vnleffe by the neceffary courfe of the hiftory I
haue bene brought to the contrary.

The manner of the Ægyptians touching the beaftes of the land. Furthermore, about the beaftes that breede
and multiplye in the region, fuche is their order.
Generally they are helde with a moft tender and
reuerent care for the mayntenaunce and fofter-
ing of them, in whiche kinde of honour (for it
is accounted a greate honour with them, to haue
regard of beaftes) the fonne euermore fucceedeth
the father. To thefe brute creatures, all fuch

as

as are refident in the cities of *Ægypt*, performe
and pay certayne vowes, makyng humble fuppli-
cation to fome one of the gods, in whofe patron-
age and protection that beaft is, which thing
they accomplifh after this manner. Shauing the
heads of their fonnes, eyther wholly, in halfe, or
for the moft parte, they waigh the hayre in
balaunce, fetting agaynft it the iuft weight in
filuer, whiche done, they deliuered it to him
that hath the charge and ouerfight of any fuche
cattell, by whom are bought heerewith fmall
peeces of fifhe which they giue the beaftes to
eate, and fuch is the meanes whereby they
nourifhe and bring them vp. The flaying of
any of thefe done of malice and fet purpofe, is
prefent death to the killer, but committed by
chaunce a mulct or peine at the difcretion and The great
arbitriment of the priefts. To kill an hauke or regard of
haukes.
the bird which is called *Ibis*, is loffe of life, in
what fort foeuer it be done. Such beafts as are
tame and come to hand, hauing their food together with men, albeit they be many in number,
yet wold they much more increafe, were it not
for the ftrange nature of cats in the countrey.
The feamale hauing once kitled, alwayes after The nature
efchueth the male, keeping her felfe fecrete of cats in
Aegypt.
and couert from him, which the *Ægyptians*
feeing, kill the kitlings, and vfe them for foode.
The

The feamale bereaued of her yong ones, and
finding her neft empty, is by that meanes
brought to fubmitte hir felfe to the bucke,
beeing of all creatures moft defirous of increafe. In time of fire, or fuche like misfortune, the cats are mooued with a certaine diuine
kind of fury and infpiration. For the *Ægyptians* behauing themfelues fecurely in the appeaf-
ing and extinguifhing the flame, the cats lie
couertly in waight, and fodenly courfing towards
the place, mount and fkip quite ouer the heads
of the people into the fire, at which chaunce
whenfoeuer it commeth to paffe, the *Ægyptians*
are extreamely forrowfull. In what houfe foeuer
Mourning
for the death
of cats and
dogs. there dies a cat, all of the fame family fhaue their
eyebrowes; but if a dog dye, their head and
body. A cat dying, is folemnely caryed to the
temple, where being well powdered with falte,
fhe is after buried in the city of *Balaftis.* A
Houndes
greatly re-
garded. bitch is euermore buryed in the fame city where
fhe dieth, yet not without the honour of a facred
tombe, burying their dogges after the fame fort,
and chiefly houndes of the malekinde, whiche
they moft of all others efteeme and fet by.
Likewife fmall ferpents called in their tongue
Mygalæ, and haukes of all kinde, if they fortune
to dye, they take and bury them at the city
Butis. Beares, fuch as be halowed, and wolues
not

not much bigger then foxes, are couered in the
fame place, where they be found dead. The
nature alfo of the Crocodyle is thys. Foure The nature
monethes in the yeare, and chiefly in the winter codyle.
feafon it liues without meate. And albeit it haue
feete like a land-beaft, yet hath it a nature middle
and indifferent, liuing as well in the water as
one drie land. Her egges fhe layes on the fhore,
where alfo fhe couereth and hatcheth the fame,
biding the moft part of the day abroade on the
dry land, but all the night tyme in the water,
being much more hoate then the cold deawe that
falleth in the night. Of all creatures I iudge
none of fo fmall and flender a beginning, to
waxe to fuch huge and infinite greatneffe, the
egge at the firft not much bigger then a goofe
egge, which meafure the broode it felfe exceed-
eth not when it fyrft commes out of the fhell,
howbeit, in durance of time, it growes to bee
monftrous, furmounting the length of feauenteene A cubite is
cubites. The Crocodyle hath eyes like a fwine, an halfe.
teeth of paffing bigneffe, accordyng to the meafure and proportion of her bodye, extendyng and
bearyng outwarde, beeyng alfo very rough and
grating lyke a fawe : and of all other creatures
is only without a tongue : the felfefame, con- The Croco-
trary to the nature and property of all other tongue.
beaftes, hath the neathermoft chap ftedfaft and
                                                    without

without moouing, and champeth her foode with
the vpper iawe. Her clawes are very ftrong and
great, a fcaly fkynne, and aboute the backe
impenetrable, that no weapon be it neuer fo
fharpe can pearce it. In the water as blinde as
a moale, on lande of an excellente fharpe and
quicke fight. Liuing in the water, it commeth
to paffe that her mouth is euermore full of
horfeleaches. No foule or beaft can abide to
The bird Trochilus. fee or come nye a Crocodile, faue only the bird
Trochilus, with whome fhe is at a continuall
truce for the fingular commodity fhe receyueth
by him. For the Crocodile at what time fhe
forfaketh the water, and commeth out on lande,
her quality is with wide and opened mouth to
lye gaping toward the Weft, whome the bird
Trochilus efpying, flyeth into her mouth, and
there deuoureth and eateth vp the horfeleaches,
which bringeth fuch pleafure to the ferpent,
that without any hurt in the world fhe fuffereth
the bird to do what fhe will. To fome of the
Ægyptians Crocodiles are in place of holy creatures, to other prophane and noyfome, which
chace and purfue them as moft odious and peftilent beaftes. Thofe that geue honour to them,
are fuch as inhabite about *Thebes*, and the poole
A tame Crocodyle. of *Mæris*, who are wont commonly to traine vp
a Crocodyle to hand, and make it tame, being
in

in all poyntes fo gentle and tractable as a dogge.
At whofe eares they hang gemmes of fingulare
price, likewife golden eareings, hampering a
chayne to the forefeete. This tame one they
cherifh and bryng vp with great care, fetting
very much by it while it liueth, and being dead,
they powder the body with fault, and lay it
vnder the ground in a veffell accounted holy.
Unlike to thefe are the people dwelling at
Elephantina, who be fo farre from thinking fo
reuerently of fuche venemous ferpents, that for
hate they flay, and in difdayne eate them. The
Ægyptians call them not Crocodyles, but Crocodiles
Champfi, this name being brought vp by the in Aegypt
people of *Ionia*, for that in fhape they re- Champfi.
femble thofe Crocodyles which amongft them
ingender and breede in hedges. Diuers are
the meanes whereby they are taken, yet amongft
other deuyfes this one feemeth to mee moft
worthy reherfall. Such as laye for them and
feeke all wayes to take them, bayte their
hookes with Swynes flefh and caft it into the The maner
myddeft of the ryuer: immediately ftanding on Crocodyles.
the fhore they beate a younge porkling and caufe
it to cry exceedingly : which the Crocodile hearing followeth the cry, and drawing neere to the
place, findeth the bayte and fwalloweth it vp at
one morfel. Being faft intangled and drawne to
lande,

lande, they firſt blinde and ſtop vp hir eyes with clay and rubbiſhe, which cauſeth hir to lye ſtill and ſuffer all thinges quietly, which otherwiſe they coulde neuer obtaine and come by without much a doe.   Likewiſe, the Ryuerhorſe (a beaſt

ſo called) in all the borders of *Papremis* is reputed holy : being of this ſhape and figure.   He hath foure feete clouen in ſunder, and houed like an Oxe : a flat noſe : and taile and Mane like an Horſe : teeth apparaunt and ſtanding out : in ſounde and cry neighing ſo like a horſe as may be : in bigneſſe refembling a mighty Bull, of ſo groſſe and thicke an hyde that being well dryed, they make thereof Darts of exceeding ſtrength and ſtiffneſſe.   There be alſo founde to breede in the ryuer certaine beaſtes much like a Beuer and liue like an Otter, which in *Ægypt* are of great accounte and thought holy.   In the ſame degre of ſacred honour are all kinde of ſcale fiſhe and Eeles.   Such is alſo their opinion and reuerance towards birds and fowles of the ayre, as wilde Geeſe and ſuch like.   There is alſo an other bird of whom aboue all other they

think moſt diuinely, called a *Phœnix;* which I neuer ſaw, but protrayed and ſhadowed in coloures.   For ſhe commeth very ſeldome into that countrey (as farre as I could heare ſay by the *Heliopolitans*) to wit, once in 500 yeares, and

that

that alſo when hir parent or breeder dyeth. If
ſhe be truely drawne by the *Ægyptians* this is The ſhape of a Phœnix.
hir forme and bigneſſe : hir feathers partly red
and partly yealow, glittering like Golde : in forme
and quantity of the body not much differing from
an Eagle. Of this *Phœnix, Egyptians* haue
bruted a ſtraunge tale, which I can hardly credit :
ſaying that the *Phœnix* flying from *Aralia*, to The nature of the Phœnix.
the temple of the Sunne in *Ægypt,* carieth in
hir tallaunts the corps of hir dead ſire, embaulmed
and roled in Myrrhe, which ſhe accuſtometh to
bury in that place. Adding alſo the maner
whereby ſhe inureth hir ſelfe to cary ſo great a
burthen. Firſt ſhe gathers a great quantity of
Myrrhe and works it into a lumpe, as much as
ſhee canne well beare, whereby to make tryall of
hir owne ſtrength. After this perceyuing hir-
ſelfe able to weylde it, ſhee maketh an hole with
hir Beake in the ſide of the balle, framing it
very hollow and empty within, wherein ſhe
incloſeth the body of hir breeder. This done,
and the hole cunningly filled vp againe, ſhe
poyſeth the whole maſſe in hir tallaunts : and
finally, ſhe tranſporteth it to *Heliopolis* to the
temple Pallace of the *Sunne :* ſo ſkilfully hand-
ling hir cariage, that the Myrrhe body and all
waygheth no more then the whole balle did
before.

This

Serpents
haunting in
Ægypt. This they mention as concerning the *Phœnix*.
Knowe wee befides, that in the region of *Thebs*
in *Ægypt,* there vfe to haunte a kinde of Serpents, had in dyuine worfhippe: of body fmale,
and nothing noyfome or hurtfull to men. Thefe
haue two hornes growing out of their heads,
and euermore dying are laide in *Iupiters* temple,
vnto whom they are holy and confecrate.

In *Arabia* there lyeth a place of no great diftaunce from the city *Batis*, whether I went of
purpofe, hauing heard of certayne wynged Serpents there to bee feene. And being come: I
behelde the ribbes and bones of Serpents in
number welnigh infinite and not to bee reckoned
whereof fome were greater, and fome leife. The
place where the bones are layde, is a fmale and
narrowe bottome betweene two Fountaynes,
opening into a wyde and wafte champion.

The bird
Ibis. The fpeach goeth, that out of *Arabia* at the
poynte of the Sprynge, many hydious and ter-
rible Serpentes take their flight into *Ægypt:*
which the fowles called *Ibides* meeting with,
ftraight wayes kill and deuour them: by which
meanes the foile is rid and deliuered of a great
plague. For this caufe the bird *Ibis* (whereto
the *Arabians* likewyfe accorde) is had in great
price and eftimation of the *Ægyptians*. The
fafhion and protrayture of this bird is fuch: hir

feathers

feathers as black as Ieat: long fhanks like a The fhape of Ibis.
Crane : an hooked beake : much about the big-
nes of a Daker hen. And in this forte is the
fowle *Ibis* rightly figured, that killeth the Serpentes as they come into the land. There is
alfo another of thefe which are brought vp, and
liue amongft men, hauing a fmale head, a flender
necke, white plumed in all partes of the body,
fauing in the head and necke, the hinder parte
of the wyngs and the taile, which are of a dark
and black hue : the legges and byll in all poynts
like the other. The Serpents themfelues in
forme and making are much like to the peftilent
and infectious beaft *Hydra,* that liueth in the Hydra a water Serpent.
water. They haue wyngs not of feathers, but
of fmothe and naked fkin like vnto the wings of
a Bat or Reremoufe. But let it fuffice vs hytherto
to haue continued the difcourfe and hyftory of
fuch beaftes as with this people are had in chiefe
and principall honour, exhibiting towards them
a certayne religious, holy, and diuine worfhip.

Now it behoueth vs to know that fuch of the
Ægyptians as dwell in the corne Countrey, and
are moft of all conuerfant in defcrying to the The chiefe parte of Ægypt, and their maners.
pofterity the acts and affayres of auncient
memory, and of all the nation the moft famous
and principall. Whofe kinde of lyuing is after
this maner. Thrife euery moneth they cleanfe
and

and purifie them felues, both vpwards by vomit-
ting and downewards by purginge : hauing efpeciall regarde of their health and welfare : euermore fuppofing all maladies and difeafes to grow
and arife of the meate which they eate. For
otherwife the *Ægyptians* are of all men liuing the
moft founde and healthfull except the *Libians :*
the caufe whereof I iudge to proceede of the
immutable and conftant courfe of the yeare,
which with them neuer varieth but falleth out
alwayes alike : the greateft caufe of defect and
Sickneffe
proceedeth
of the
vnfeafonable
times of the
yeare. fickneffe in men, aryfing of the chaung and
mutability of the fame. Their bread is con-
tinually made of fine wheat : their wyne for the
moft part compound of barley : the country
bearing no vynes at all. They liue by fifh partly
raw and dryed agaynft the funne : fometimes
powdred with falt. Likewife by raw byrds well
falted, as Quayles, Duckes, and other fmale
fowle. In like maner, of other Creatures that
haue neere affinity either with fifh or fowle they
make their prouifion and furniture, rofting fome
and boyleing other. The rych and wealthy men
of the lande in greate affemblies haue an vfuall
cuftome, that by fome in the company there
fhoulde bee caryed aboute in a fmale coffine the
liuely and expreffe image of a deade man one
or two cubits in length, which hauing fhewne

and

and revealed to all that are prefente, hee fayth *An excellent*
cuftome
thus: Beholde here, and amiddeft thy pleafure *practyfed by*
Nobles of
and delighte remember this, for fuch a one after *Ægypt.*
thy death fhalt thou bee thy felfe. Such is their
order in feaftes and banquets, contenting them
felues alwayes with the cuftomes of their owne
countrey and refufing to be ruled by ftraunge
and forraine maners. Amongft whom are diuerfe *New*
fafhions
fafhions, very conuenient and well appoynted: *abhorred.*
in the number of thefe an excellente Poeme or
Ditty, which the *Grekes* call *Lynus.* And in
truth meruayling at other thinges in *Ægypt*, I
am not a litle amazed at this, whence the name
of *Lynus* fhould come. The Songe they feeme
to haue kept and retained from all antiquity.
Lynus in the *Ægyptian* gibberifhe is called
Maneros, who (as they fay) being the onely
fonne of their firfte Kinge, was furprifed and
taken away by vntimely death, whom the
Ægyptians bewayle and lament in this pitious
and dolefull verfe. Herein they iumpe and
agree with the *Lacedæmonians*, in that the in- *Ciuility.*
feriour meeting with his elder, yeeldeth the
way, and fheweth him a dutifull obeifaunce in
rifeing from his feate, if happily hee bee fitting
as he paffeth by: in which poynte they are
vnlike all the reft of the *Grecians* befides. Meet-
inge in the way in place of mutuall falutation,
they

they vſe humble and curteous reuerence each towarde other, bendinge their hands to each others knees. Commonly they goe clothed in linnen garments made faſt with a lace about the thigh, which kinde of attyre they call *Calaſyris :* ouer this they caſt alſo another veſture of linnen very cleane and white. Garments of woollen are neuer caried into the houſes of religion, neither will any man ſhrowd him ſelfe in a woollen veſture, which is accounted prophane. This hath ſome agreement with the ceremonies vſually kept in the ſacred feaſts of *Bacchus* and *Orpheus,* which partly were taken from the *Ægyptians,* and partly deuiſed by the *Pythagoreans.* For ſuch as haue bene partakers of thoſe ryts, haue euermore abhorred to be buried in woollen garments. Whereof alſo an holy reaſon is geuen which we dare not diſcloſe. Many other thinges haue bene invented by the *Ægyptians,* as what day and moneth is proper and appertinent to euery god. Likewiſe in *Aſtrology* what fortune is incident to him that is borne one ſuch a day, how hee ſhall proue in lyfe, by what meanes hee ſhall miſcary by death : which thinges haue bene vſed of many that haue laboured in the Arte and Science of *Poëtry.*

Alſo, more wonders, and ſtraunge ſightes and euentes haue bene diſcuſſed and interpreted by them,

Pythagoreans were ſuch as allowed the doctrine of Pythagoras Philoſophy.

The Ægyptians firſt inuented the arte to read a man's deſtiny.

them, then by any other Nation liuinge. For
as any fuch thing hath happened at any tyme
they commit it to memory, awaighting dilli-
gently what iffue it hath: and if the like fall
out at any time after, they coniecture of the ende
and effect thereof by the example of the firft.
The knowledge of diuination is fo practifed by
them, that they impute not the inuention thereof
to the will of men, but to certayne of the gods.
In their lande there bee thefe Oracles. The
prophecy of *Hercules, Apollo, Minerua, Diana,* The feates
Mars, and *Iupiter,* moft of all reuerencing the in Ægypt.
diuine feate of *Latona,* helde at the city *Batis.*
Thefe prophefies are not all inftituted after the
fame fafhion, but haue a difference and diuerfity
betweene them. Phificke is fo ftudyed and practyfed with them that euery difeafe hath his
feuerall phifition, who ftryueth to excell in heal-
ing that one difeafe, and not to be expert in
curinge many: whereof it commeth that euery
corner is full of Phyfitions. Some for the eyes, In Ægypt
other for the head, many for the teeth, not a hath his
fewe for the ftomacke and belly. Finally, fuch phyfition.
as are of knowledge to deale with fecret and
priuy infirmities.

In like forte, the maner of mourninge, and
funerall forrow at the death of friendes: alfo the
maner of fepulture and buryall which they vfe,

is

Of mourning
and burying
the dead. is moſt worthy memory. When as any of their familiars or domeſticall friendes fortune to deceaſe, (bee hee of regarde amongſt them) all the women of that family beſmere and gryme their heads and faces with myre and droſſe: and leauing the forlorne and languiſhed corps amongeſt their friends and acquaintaunce, they themſelues being ſtraight gyrded, with their breaſts all bare and naked, accompanied with al the women of their kindred, wander about the ſtreets with moſt piteous lamentation and howling: on the other ſide, the men faſt gyrte about the loynes, thump and beate themſelues, as the moſt miſerable, infortunate, and wretched perſons in the world. After this they cary out the body to embalme and preſerue. Certaine there be definitly appointed for the ſame purpoſe, that make an occupation and trade hereof. Theſe when the corſe is brought vnto them, propounde The maner
of embalm-
ing the dead. and ſhew to the bringers, ſundry formes and pictures of the dead, paynted or carued in wood, one of which is wrought with moſt curiouſe arte and workmanſhip (which we thinke impiety to name): the ſecond of leſſe pryce: the third meaneſt of all: demaundinge of the bringers, to which of theſe paterns and examples their friend ſhal be dreſſed. Being agreed of the price they depart, leauing the body with the ſalyners: who incontinent

incontinent feafon and preferue the corps with
al induftry, drawing the braynes out by the
nofthrills with a croked inftrument of Iron, in
place whereof they fill the Brayne pan with
moft fweete and pleafaunt oyntments. This
done and finifhed, they cut and rip vp the
Bowells with a fharp ftone of *Æthyopia,* taking
thereout the paunche and entrals, and clenfinge
the belly with wyne of Palme tree : fecondly,
with frefh water mingled with moft fragrant and
delightfull fpyces : in place hereof they force and
ftuffe the belly it felfe with myrrhe, of the fineft
forte brayed and pounded in a morter. Likewife, with *Caffia* and all kinde of pleafaunt
odours, except frankincenfe. Hauing thus done,
they fowe it vp agayne, and embalming the body,
preferue it for the terme of 70 dayes : longer
then which they may not keepe it. The dayes
exfpired and drawne to an ende, they take the
corfe and wafh it ouer a frefh, annoynting the
body with gum (which is to the *Ægyptians* in
fteede of Glue) and attyring it in a fine lynen
drawne together with a lace, they send him back
againe to his friends. His friends in the tyme,
while the faliners haue him in hand, procure an
Image to be made to the likenes and refem-
blaunce of him that is dead, wherein being
holow and vauted within, they caufe him to be
inclofed,

inclofed, layinge both the Image and the body
therein contayned in a toumbe together. Howbeit they which in meaner eftate and fortune
cannot reach fo high, order the bodyes of their
frindes in forme as followeth. Firft of all
they fill a clyfter with the oyntment of neder
which without any maner cuttinge or opening
the belly, they ftrayne it into the body by the
inferiour partes and Fundament, preferninge the
corfe as before, 70 dayes. The laft day of all
they dreyne out the oyle from the bowels of the
dead : which is of fuch vertue, that it bringeth
out with it all the inner parts of the belly cor-
rupted and feftered. Herewith alfo they inftil
and power into the body Saltpeter, which is of
force to depraue, taynt, and confume the flefh,
leauing nothing but fkin and bones : which
done, they eftfones deliuer the body to the
owners. There is alfo a third kinde of vfage
accuftomably practifed about the bodyes of the
dead : that if any one be deceafed whofe friendes
are very poore and of fmaleft fubftaunce, they
only purge the belly, and preferuing the corps
with falt for terme of like time as before, in fine,
redeliuer him to the bringers.

The wyues of noble men, and fuch as are very
fayre and of great refpect for their beauty, are
not prefently vpon pointe of their death, geuen

to

to be embalmed, but three or foure dayes after, Fayre gentle-women dying are kept three dayes before they be pre-serued.
fearing leaft they fhould be abufed by the inor-
dinate luft of fuch as dreffe them : alleadging
moreover, that a Saliner fometimes working
fuch abufe vpon the dead body of a woman, was
taken in the maner, and his villany difcryed by
one of his owne company. If it fortune any one
either of the *Ægyptians*, or of forraine countries
to be drowned and caft on fhore, the City in
whofe borders he is founde muft fuftaine the
charge of the funeralles, which in honorable
maner muft be executed, and the body buried
in the facred and holy Monumentes. Being not
lawfull for his friends and allies any whit to
intermeddle or touch the dead, but the Priefts
affigned to the worfhip of the ryuer *Nylus* in-
toumbe and bury him fo nicely and folemnly as
if it were the body of a god. The cuftomes of
Greece they will in no wife follow : vtterly
eftraunging them felues from all orders borowed
and deryued from other Nations.

Albeit *Chemmis* a great City in the Prouince The City Chemmis.
of *Thebs* not farre from the city *Nëa*, wherein
ftandeth the Temple of *Perfeus*, fonne of *Danäe*,
built fourefquare and incompaffed rounde aboute
wyth a Springe or Groue of Date trees : hauing
alfo a large entry of ftone, on each fide whereof
are placed two Images of paffing greatneffe :
within

F

within the pallace is contayned the carued monument of *Perfeus*, whom the *Chemmyts* auouch
often times to appeare vnto them out of the
earth, and not feldome in the church : at which
time they find his flipper which he was wonte
to weare, two cubytes in length : affyrminge
that at fuch times as that is feene, the yeare
proueth very fertile and profperous throughe out
all *Ægypt*. This towne (I fay) hath ordayned
certayne games of exercife in the honour of
Perfeus, after the maner of *Greece*. Thefe
being demaunded of mee why *Perfeus* fhould
appeare to them alone, and for what caufe in
the celebration of their games, they diffented
from the reft of the *Ægyptians :* they made
anfwere, that *Perfeus* was iffued of theyr city,
adding moreuver, that *Daneus* and *Lynæus*
were alfo *Chemmyts* and fayled into *Greece :* in
blafing whofe Pedagree they came at length
to *Perfeus*, who comming into *Ægypt* for the
felfe fame caufe as the *Grecians* teftify, namely,
to fetch the head of *Gorgon* out of *Africk*, came
alfo to them and called to remembraunce his
kinred and linage, of whom hauing taken ac-
quayntaunce, and hearing his mother to fpeake
of the name of *Chem*, he inftituted a game of all
exercifes, which according to his appointment
and firft ordinaunce they obferue till this day.
                                                    Thefe

Thefe are the maners of thofe that lye aboue the
Fennes, fuch as dwell in the Maryfes differ not
from the reft, neither in other things, nor in
eftate of mariage, euery one inioying the priuate
fellowſhip of his owne wyfe, in femblable maner
to the *Grecians.* Notwithſtanding for the eafie
prouifion of their foode and fuſtenaunce other
thinges haue bene foughte out and deuifed by
them. For in time of the floude when the Their floud
ryuer ouergoeth the countrey, there arife in the in Ægypt.
water great plenty of lyllyes, which the people
of *Ægypt* call *Lotos.* Thefe they reape and
dry them in the Sunne. The feede whereof
(growing in the middeft of the flower, fomewhat
like vnto Popy feede) they boyle, after which
they kneade it into cakes, and bake it for breade.
The roote of this is very tothfome, pleafant and
good to eate : being of forme very rounde, and
in bigneſſe like an aple. There is alfo another
kinde of lyllyes much like to rofes, which in like
maner haue their growth in the water, from
whofe roote fprings a bud vnlike to the former,
bearing fruite in maner and likeneſſe of an hony
Combe: herein are contayned certayne fmale
kernells refembling the ftone of an Olyue, not
vnfit for fuſtenance, and commonly eaten of the
Ægyptians, afwell frefh as wythered. The felfe
fame people when the feafon of the yeare ferueth,
are

are bufily conuerfant in gathering a kinde of
Rufh called *Byllus*, the top whereof they crop
and turne it into vfe of foode : the refidue being
much about one cubyte in length, they partly
eate and partly fell. Such as be defirous to
make fine and delicate meate of this Rufh, vfe
to caft it into an Ouen and broyle it : fome there
be that lyue only by fifh, which hauing taken,
they incontinently draw them and parch them in
the Sunne like ftockfifh, and being well dryed

The nature
of their fifh.

they eate them. The common forte of fifh vfed
among them, breede not in the ryuer, but in
pooles, being of this nature. Toward the time
of fpawning they leaue the fennes and make
repayre generally to the fea, the male fifhes in
maner of captaines leading the ranke. Thefe
male fifhe as they paffe ftill onwarde fhed theyr
feede by the way, which their femals following
after immediatly deuour, and thereof fhortly
after breede theyr fpawnes. Now at the pointe
of breede, the femals forfaking the falt waters,
ftower backe agayne to the maryfes to their
accuftomed haunte, leadinge the males that follow after them : and in fwiming backe agayne,
they voide fpawne, being very fmale cornes,
like the graynes of muftard feede which lighting
upon the male fifhe in the tayle of the rancke,
are fwallowed vp and deuoured by them. Not
one

one of thefe litle graynes but will grow to a
fifhe, as well may bee feene by thofe that efcape
the males, and are vndeuoured: which being
nourifhed by the waters growe to fmale Frye.
Such of thefe fifhes as are taken fwimminge to
the fea, are founde to haue the left fide of theyr
heads very much worne and gauled: and in
comming from the fea, the right side: the caufe
being this, that both in going and comming they
continually grate agaynft the fhore and bancks
of the ryuer, as a direction to them in paffinge
to and fro, leaft that floting in the middeft of
the ftreame, they chaunce to ftray and wander
ont of the right courfe. At fuch time as the
ryuer *Nilus* beginneth to fwell, all the lowe
places in the countrey and Ponds neere adioyning
to the ryuer doe likewife increafe: being then
to bee feene great ftore of younge Fry in euery
litle puddle: whereof thefe fhould breede, this
feemeth to be a probable caufe. That the yeare
before, at the fall and decreafe of the water, the
fifh which together with the ryuer departe them
felves, leaue behinde them their fpawne in the
mudde, which at the ryfing of the nexte floude,
being eftfones moyftned, by the waters, recouer
vertue, and growe to bee fifh. As touchinge
which thinges let it feeme fufficient thus much
to haue fpoken.

The

The gathering of fruite for oyles. The *Ægyptians* that keepe in the fenne countrey, vfe a certaine oyle made of a tree, which the *Apothecaryes* call *Palmachri*. Thefe trees (that fpringe naturally in *Greece*) the *Ægyptians* accuftome to plant and fet by the banckes of Pooles and ryuers, which is the caufe that they beare fruite, but very ftrong and rancke of fauoure. The fruite being gathered, fome of them bruife it againft the fyre, other fome frie it in a pan, referuing that which commeth of it, which ferueth them partly for Oyle, partly for the vfe of their Lamps and candles, yeelding (as they fayd before) a deyne very loathfome and vnfauory. Likewife, agaynft gnats and flyes, wherewith their lande aboundeth aboue meafure, certaine remedies are founde out by them. Such as dwell aboue the Fennes are holpen herein by towers and high garrets, wherein they take their fleepe, forafmuch as the winde will not fuffer the Gnats to fly high. The people of the Fennes in fteede of Turrets are fayne to worke this deuife. Each man hath his Nets, wherewith in the day time they goe on fifhing, and in the night pytche them aboute their chambers wherein they reft, by whych meanes they come to take a nappe of nyne houres longe: whereas otherwife (were they neuer fo well wrapped in clothes) the Gnats with their fharp nebbes would

pierc

pierc and ftinge quite through all, being not
able in like maner to paffe through the Nets.
Their Shippes vfed for burthen or caryage are The maner
made of a kinde of Thorne, not farre vnlike the Shyps.
tree *Lotos* growing in *Cyrene*, from the which
there iffueth a certayne kinde of gumme. Of
the body of this thorne they fawe and fquare out
certaine boardes two cubits longe, and fafhioned
like a tilefheard, which they frame and compact
together after this maner. Firft they vnite and
ioyne the plancks together with an infinit number
of nayles and pynnes, binding the fame to many
tranfomes that goe both croffe and longe wayes
for the ftrength of the veffell. Their wood they
frame not in compaffe, after the maner of other
Nations, but faften and knit the ioyntes together
with Bullrufhes and fuch like. They haue only
one Helme or Sterne, which is made to goe
throughe the hinder parte of the Shippe. The
Maft is likewife of thorne, the Sayle of the
Rufhe *Byllus*. Thefe kinde of veffells are not
able to cut againft the ftreame, but are haled
and drawne forward by land. Downe the
ftreame they paffe in this wyfe. They frame an
hurdle of the bufhe *Tamarifk*, faft bounde and
tyed together with the peelings of greene Cane
or Reedes: prouydinge moreouer a mighty ftone
wyth an hole through the middeft, two talents
in

in weight: which done, they caſt the hurdle
into the ſtreame beinge made faſt with a Rope
to the noſe of the Veſſell: contrariwiſe, the
ſtonne they tye behynde wyth an other Cable,
geuinge it ſo much ſcope that it may ſinke to the
bottome. By which meanes it commeth to paſſe
that the ſtreame caryinge on the hurdle, cauſeth
the Shippe to follow, with exceedinge ſwift-
neſſe and the ſtone on the other ſide drayling
behinde, directeth the ſame in euen and ſted-
faſt courſe. At ſuch time as the ryuer ouerrun-
neth the ſoyle, the Cityes are only apparent and
vncouered, reſembling in ſhew the Iſles of the
ſea *Ægêum,* all the land beſides being in maner
of a ſea. The Cities which in time of the floud
are extante, be in place of Portes for the ſhips to
lye at rode in. During which time they ſayle
not in the mayne ryuer, but through the midſt
of the fieldes. They that take ſhipping from
the Citye *Naucrates* to *Memphis,* haue their
courſe by the *Pyramides:* albeit there be another way alſo tendinge to the ſame place,
ſtrykinge ouer by the Neb of *Delta,* and the
City of the *Cercaſians.* Likewiſe as we take
our voyage from the Sea coaſte, and the city
Canobus to *Naucrates* through the wyde and
open fieldes, we ſhall paſſe by *Anthylla* a towne
ſo named : in like manner arryuinge, at the city
Arcandry.

The Pyra-
mides were
certayne
long towers
of ſtone.

Arcandry. Anthylla a city of chiefe renowne, is euermore geuen and allotted by the Kinge of *Ægypt* to his Queene, that then is, to finde her fhoes, which are purchafed by the reuenewes of the fame. Which cuftome hath remayned fince the tyme that the *Perfians* gouerned in *Ægypt.* *Archandry* feemeth to haue taken the name of *Archander,* fonne in lawe to *Danæus,* and the lawfull ofspringe of *Phthius Achæus:* not denying but that there might bee another befides him: but howfoeuer it is, the city *Archandry* can in no wyfe be made an *Ægyptian* name. Hytherto haue I fet downe fuch thinges as eyther by my felfe I haue feene and knowne: or bene conftantly aduertyfed thereof by the people of the region, determining henceforth to profecute fuch matters, as I haue onely by herefay, interlaceing the fame otherwhiles, with fuch thinges as of myne owne knowledge I am able to iuftifie.

Menes the firfte Kinge of *Ægypt* (as the pryefts make reporte) by altering the courfe of the ryuer, gayned all that grounde whereon the City *Memphis* is fituated : the floud being wonte before time to haue his courfe faft by the fandy mountayne which lyeth towarde *Lybia.* This *Menes* therefore damminge vppe the bofome of the ryuer towardes the fouth Region

hauinge

hauinge caſt vppe a pyle, or bulwarke of Earth
much after an hundred Furlonges aboue the
City, by that meanes dryed the old Chanell,
cauſinge the ryuer to forſake and abandone his
naturall courſe and runne at randame amiddeſt
the hills. To which damme alſo the *Perſians* that
rule in *Ægypte* euen at this day haue a dilligent
eye : yearely fortifyinge and repayringe the ſame
wyth newe and freſh Earth. Through the which
if by fortune the ryuer ſtryuinge to recouer his
olde courſe, ſhould happily make a breach, the
city *Memphis* were in daunger to bee ouerwhelmed
with water. By the ſelfe ſame *Menes* firſte bear-
inge rule and authority in *Ægypt* (after that by
turning the ſtreame of *Nilus* he had made dry
ground of that where erſt the ryuer had his paſſage) in the ſame plot of land was the city it ſelfe
founded and erected, which (as well may bee
ſeene) ſtands in the ſtraight and narrow places
of the countrey. More then this, to the North
and Weſt (for Eaſtward *Memphis* is bounded
by the courſe of the riuer) hee cauſed to be
drawne out of the ryuer a large and wyde poole :
beinge alſo the founder of *Vulcans* temple in
Memphis, one of the fayreſt buildinges and of
chiefeſt fame in all the countrey of *Ægypte.*
Three hundred and thirty Prynces that by mutuall
ſucceſſion followed *Menes,* the prieſts alſo readily
mentioned

mentioned out of the books of their Monuments: of which number 18 were by Countrey *Æthyo-* *pians*, and one a forraine and outlandifh woman, whofe nation they knew not, al the reft being fprong of their owne land. This woman that afpired to the crowne, bare the name of the famous Queene of *Babylon*, and was called *Nitocris:* whofe brother in the time of his empire being flaine by the *Ægyptians*, *Nitocris* wearing the crowne after him fought meanes fecretly how to revenge his death, which fhe brought to paffe by a ftraunge deuice and pollicy. Hauing therefore builte for hir owne vfe a fayre and gorgeous courte, fhe caufed an hollow Vaut or caue to be caft vnder the earth, pretending for the time a reafon of hir deuice, albeit farre different from hir fecret minde and purpofe. The work ended, fhe inuited thither the moft part of hir nobles to a banquet, fuch as fhee knew to haue bene the authors and workers of hir brothers death, who being all affembled and fet together in an inner Parlour, expectinge their cheere, the water was let in at a priuy grate and ouerwhelmed them all.

Thefe thinges they fpake of *Nitocris*, adding befides, that hauing wrought this feate, fhee caft hir felfe into an houfe full of Afhes to efcape vnpunifhed.

By

Mœris the
laſt of the
330 prynces. By the reſt of the kinges of *Ægypt* the prieſtes coulde recyte no glorious acte that ſhoulde bee accompliſhed, ſauing by the noble king *Mœris* the laſt and lateſt of all this crewe. To whom they attribute the building of the great porches belonging to *Vulcans* temple, ſtanding on the North parte of the Pallace. By the fame alſo was a certaine fenne delued and caſt vp, wherein were builded certaine mighty Towers called *Pyramides*, of whoſe bygneſſe, as alſo of the large compaſſe and amplitude of the Poole, wee will ioyntely intreate in another place.

Theſe thinges were done by *Mœris* the laſt king. The reſt conſuminge the time of their raygne in ſilence and obſcurity, whom for the ſame cauſe I will paſſe ouer, and addreſſe my ſpeache to him who came after them in time and went before them in Dignity: namely, the

Sefoſtris
king in
Ægypt, and
his exploy ts. worthy Prynce *Seſoſtris*. Him the Pryeſtes recounte firſte of all the kings of *Ægypt* to haue paſſed the narrow Seas of *Arabia* in longe Ships or Gallyes, and brought in ſubiection to the Crowne all thoſe People that marche a longe the redde Sea. From whence retyringe backe againe the ſame way, hee came and gathered a greate power of men, and tooke his paſſage ouer the waters into the mayne lande, conquering and ſubduing all Countreyes whether ſo euer hee

went

went. Such as hee founde valiaunte and hardye
not refufinge to ieoparde their fafety in the defence and maynetenaunce of their liberty, after
the victory obtayned, hee fixed in theyr countrey
certayne fmale pyllers or Croffes of ftone, wherein
were ingrauen the names of the kinge and the
countrey, and how by his owne proper force and
puiffaunce he had made them yelde. Contrarywyfe, fuch as without controuerfie gaue them- A monument
felues into his handes, or with litle ftryfe and proch of
leffe bloudfhed were brought to relent: with Cowardife.
them alfo, and in their region he planted Pillers
and builte vp litle croffes, as before, wherein
were carued and importrayed the fecret partes of
women, to fignifie to the pofterity the bafe and
effeminate courage of the people there abyding.
In this forte hee trauayled with his army vp and
downe the mayne, paffing out of *Afia* into *Europe*,
where he made conqueft of the *Scythians* and
Thracians: which feemeth to haue been the
fartheft poynt of his voyage: for fo much as
in their land alfo his titles and marks are ap-
parantly feene, and not beyonde. Herefro
hee began to meafure his fteps back agayne
incamping his powre at the ryuer *Phafis:*
where, I am not able to difcuffe, whether king
Sefoftris him felfe planted any parte of his army
in that place euer after to poffeffe that countrey:

or

or whether fome of his fouldiers wearyed with continuall perigrination and trauayle, toke vp their manfion place and refted there. For the

The people Colchi fprong of the Ægyptians. people named *Colchi*, feeme to be *Ægyptians:* which I fpeake rather of myne owne gathering, then of any other mans information. Howbeit, for tryall fake commoninge with the inhabitants of either nation, the *Colchans* feemed rather to acknowledge and remember the *Ægyptians*, then the *Ægyptians* them: affyrming, that the *Colchans* were a remnante of *Sefoftris* army. Myfelfe haue drawne a coniecture hereof: that both people are in countenance a like black, in hayre a like fryzled, albeit it may feeme a very feeble geffe, the fame being alfo in other nations. A better furmife may be gathered of this, that the people of *Æthyopia*, *Ægypt*, and *Colchis* only of all men, circumcyfe and cut of the fore-fkin from their hidden partes, reteyning the cuftome time out of minde. For the *Phœnicians* and *Syrians* that dwell in *Palæftina*, confeffe themfelues to haue borrowed the maner of cir-cumficion from the *Ægyptians*. And as for thofe *Syrians* that dwell neere vnto the ryuers *Thermodon* and *Parthemus*, and the people called *Macrones* their next neighbours, they tooke the felfe fame vfe and cuftome of the *Colchans*. Howbeit, the *Ægyptians* and *Æthyopians*, which

of

of them learned it of others, it is hard to difcerne, forafmuch as the cuftome in both Countryes is of great antiquity. Neverthelefle, very
good occafion of conie&ture is offred vnto vs,
that it came fyrft from the *Ægyptians,* at fuch
time as the *Æthyopians* had exchaunge of mar-
chaundife with them. For the *Phœnicians,* that
in like maner haue mutuall trafique which the
Grecians, leaue of to circumcyfe themfelues, and
refufe in that poynte to be conformable to the
lawes and ftatutes of their countrey. One thinge
more may be alleaged wherein the people of
Colchis doe very narrowly refemble the cuftomes
of *Ægypt,* in fo much as, thefe two nations
alone, work their lynnen and drefle theyr flax
after the fame forte, in all poyntes refpe&ting
each other both in order of lyfe and maner of
language. The flaxe which is brought from
Colchis the *Grecians* call *Sardonick :* the other
comming out of *Ægypt* they terme after the
name of the countrey, *Ægyptian* flaxe. But to
returne to the tytles and emblems that king
Sefoftris lefte behind him in all regions through
the which he paffed, many thereof are fallen to
decay. Notwithftanding, certaine of them in
Syria and *Palæftina* I beheld with myne own
eyes, intayled with fuch pofyes as we fpake of
before, and the pi&tures of womens fecretes in-

grauen

grauen in them. Likewife in *Ionia* are to bee feene two fundry Images of *Sefoftris* himfelfe carued in pillers : one as we paffe from *Ephefus* to *Phocæa :* another in the way from *Sardis* to *Smyrna.* Eyther of thefe haue the forme and figure of a man, fiue hands breadth in bigneffe, bearing in his righte hand a Darte, in his left a bowe, his harneffe and furniture after the manner of the *Ægyptians* and *Æthyopians.* Croffe his backe from the one fhoulder to the other went a fentence ingrauen in the holy letter of *Ægypt :* hauing this meaning. *By my owne force did I vanquifhe this region.* Notwithftandinge it is not there fpecified what he fhould be, albeit els where it is to be feene. Some haue deemed this monument to haue bene the image of *Memnon,* not a litle deceyued in opinion. This noble and victorious prince *Sefoftris* making his re-turne to *Ægypt,* came (by report of the priefts) to a place named *Daphnoe pelufiæ,* with an in-finite trayne of forraine people out of al Nations by him fubdued : where being very curteoufly met and welcomed by his brother, whom in his abfence he had lefte for Viceroy and protectour of the countrey, he was alfo by the fame inuited to a princely banquet, him felfe, his wife, and his children. The houfe whereinto they were entered, being compaffed about with dry matter,

was

Memnon the fonne of Aurora flayne in the warre at Troy.

The death of Sefoftris intended by his owne brother.

was fuddaynely by the treachery of his brother
fet on fire, which he perceiuing toke counfayle
with his wife then prefent, how to efcape and
auoyde the daunger. The woman either of a
readier wit or riper cruelty, aduifed him to caft
two of his fixe children into the fire, to make
way for him felfe and the reft to paffe: time
not fuffering him to make any long ftay, he
put his wyues counfayle in fpeedy practife, and
made a bridge through the fire of two of his
children, to preferue the reft aliue. *Sefoftris*
in this forte deliuered from the cruell treafon
and malicious deuife of his brother, firft of
all tooke reuenge of his trecherous villany
and diuelifh intent: in the next place bethink-
ing himfelfe in what affayres to beftowe the
multitude which he had brought with him,
whome afterwards he diuerfly employed: for
by thefe captiues were certayne huge and monftrous ftones rolled and drawne to the temple
of *Vulcane.* Likewife, many trenches cut out
and deriued from the riuer into moft places of
the countrey, whereby the land being aforetime The coun-
paffable by cart and horfe, was thencefoorth Ægypt cut
bereaued of that commodity: for in all the time trenches
enfuing, the countrey of *Ægypt* being for the better con-
moft parte playne and equall, is through the ueyance of
creekes and windings of the ditches brought to
                                        that

G

that paffe, that neyther horffe nor wayne can haue any courfe or paffage from one place to another. Howbeit, *Sefoftris* inuented this for the greater benefite and commodity of the lande, to the ende that fuch townes and cities as were farre remooued from the riuer, might not at the fall of the floud be pinched with the penury and want of water, which at all times they haue

A diuifion of land. deriued and brought to them in trenches. The fame King made an equall diftribution of the whole countrey to all his fubiects, allotting to euery man the lyke portion and quantitie of ground, drawne out and limited by a fourefquare fourme. Heereof the King himfelfe helde yeerely reuenewes, euery one being rated at a certayne rent and penfion, which annually he payd to the crowne, and if at the rifing of the floud it for-tuned any mans portion to be ouergone by the waters, the King was thereof aduertifed, who forthwyth fent certayne to furuey the ground, and to meafure the harmes which the floud had done him, and to leauy out the crowne rent ac-cording to the refidue of the land that remayned.

The begin-ning of Geo-metry. Heereof fprang the noble fcience of Geometry, and from thence was tranflated into *Greece.* For as touching the *Pole* and *Gnomon* (which is to fay) the rule, and the twelue partes of the day, the *Grecians* tooke them of the *Babylonians.*

This

This King *Sefoftris* held the Empyre alone,
leauing in *Æthiopia* before the temple of *Vulcane* certayne monuments to the pofteritie, to
wit, certayne images of ftone, one for hymfelfe, The images of King Sefoftris.
another for his wife, beeyng eache of them thirtie
cubites : the foure images alfo of hys foure
fonnes, beeying each of them twentie cubites
apeece. In proceffe of time when the image of
King *Darius* that gouerned *Perfia* fhould haue
bene placed before the picture of *Sefoftris*, the
prieft of *Vulcane* which ferued in the temple
woulde in no wife permit it to bee done, denying that *Darius* had euer atchieued the like
exploites that *Sefoftris* had done. Who, befides
the conquering of fundrie other nations (not inferiour in number to thofe whiche had beene
ouercome by *Darius*) had alfo brought in fub-
iection the moft couragious and valiaunt people
of *Scythia :* for whyche caufe, it were agaynft
reafon to preferre hymfelfe in place before him
vnto whome he was inferiour in chiualry,
whiche bolde aunfwere of the prieft, King
Darius tooke in good parte and brooked wel-
ynough.

Sefoftris dying, the feate imperiall came to hys The death of Sefoftris, whome Pheco fuc-ceeded.
fonne *Pheco*, who beeyng bereaued of hys fight,
vndertooke no voyage of warre, but remayned
quiet in his kingdome. The caufe he was
ftricken

ftricken blynde, is fayde to be this. At what
tyme the waters of the floud increafing, by
reafon of a mightie raging winde, had drowned
the lowe countreys eyghteene cubites deepe.
The King inraged at the vnaccuftomed fwelling
of the ryuer, tooke hys darte and difcharged it
into the middeft of the waters, for whyche hys
vnreuerent facte, the fame is, that hys fighte
incontinente was taken from hym, and hee became blynde the fpace of tenne yeares. In the
eleuenth yeare, there arofe a prophecie in the
city *Butis*, that the tyme of hys miferie was
nowe exfpyred, and that hys fyght fhoulde eftfoones be reftored agayne, if in cafe he wafhed
hys eyes in the water of a woman, whych neuer
knewe man but her owne hufbande.   For
An exquifite further proofe of thys phetie medicine, the Kyng
medicine for
the eyes.   beganne firft wyth hys owne wyfe, whych working not the effecte he looked for, he tryed many
others, but all in vayne, laftly, lighting vppon
a poore feely woman that had neuer woorfhipped
more Sainctes then one, hee fpeedely recouered
hys fighte agayne, and caufing all thofe whome
earft he had prooued to be gathered into one
citie (the name whereof was called *Reddclodd*)
he fet fire to the towne, and confumed them
all.

The King thus healed, and freely acquited of
hys

hys former miſerie, began to be deuoute, in- An army of honeſt women burnt at a clap.
creaſing the temples of the gods with giftes of
exceeding value. All which deſerue for theyr
excellencie to be had in memorie, and chiefly
thoſe that he offered in the temple of the Sunne,
which were theſe, two mighty great ſtones which
the *Ægyptians* in theyr tongue called *Obeli*, in
faſhion like a ſpit or broach 100 cubites long, and
in breadth 80.

Next after hym the kingdome deſcended to a
certayne man of the citie *Memphis*, whoſe name
in the greeke language was *Protheus*, to whome Protheus King of Ægypt.
the *Ægyptians* erected a temple, which is yet to
be ſeene in *Memphis*, very fayre and beautifull,
garniſhed wyth rich and ſingulare giftes. On
euery ſide whereof dwell the *Phenices*, a people
deſcended of the *Tyrians*, whereof the place
taketh the name, and is tearmed the tentes of
the *Tyrians*. Within the temple there is ſtand-
yng the houſe of *Proteus*, called the court of
ſtraunge *Venus*, vnder which name is meant (as
I deeme) *Helena*, the daughter of *Tyndarus*,
who as a gueſt agaynſt her wyll, kepte reſyaunce
for a tyme in the court of *Protheus*, and was
tearmed the ſtraunge *Venus*, in as much as the
other *Venus* (who hath many temples in *Ægypt*)
is neuer called by the name of ſtraunge. Heereof
entring talke with the ſacred order of the prieſtes,
they

Of the
ariuall of
Paris in
Ægypt.

A Sanctuary
for feruantes.

they difcourfed vnto me, that *Alexander* hauing ftolne *Helena* from the *Spartanes*, and fpeedyng hymfelfe homewarde by the fea called *Ægeum*, by conftraynte of weather was driuen into the *Ægyptian* feas, and perforce againfte his will, was caft afhore in *Ægypt.* His ariual was at the mouth of the floud *Nilus* called *Canobicum*, at the porte whiche the inhabitants tearme by the name of *Trachex.* In this place is fituated a temple to *Hercules*, wherevnto if any mans feruaunt or vaffall flye, and get vppon hym the holy markes (as they call them) in token that hee yeeldeth hys whole alleageaunce to the god of that place, it is not lawfull for any man to touch him, which order was kept inuiolate vnto our age. The feruauntes of *Alexander* hearing of the lawes of this temple, forfooke their Lorde, and fled vnto it, and in humble manner fub-mitting themfelues before the god, they accufed their mayfter (whofe death they all defired) fhewing in what manner he came by *Helena*, and the great iniury he had wrought to her huf-band *Menelaus.* The fame playnt alfo they framed before the priefts of *Hercules*, and the chiefe gouernour of the port named *Thonis.* *Thonis* hauing hard the accufation of thefe poore fuppliants, fent in all hafte to the King in thefe wordes: Knowe you (noble Prince) that a fewe dayes

dayes fince, a certayne ftraunger of the *Troiane* lignage (hauing committed a moft villanous acte in *Greece*, by entifing away the wife of him that had geuen him entertaynement) is by force of tempeft dryuen vpon our coaftes, we defire there- fore to knowe your hignefle pleafure, whether we fhall geue him free paffage into his countrey, or bereaue him of that he hath, and fende him awaye. To which newes the King returned an aunfwere faying. The perfon you fpeake of, of what nation foeuer hee bee whiche hathe wrought this defpitefull treacherie to his hofte, fee you apprehend and bring to my court, to the ende I may heare what he can fay for himfelfe. Whereat *Thonis* without any farther delibera- tion, tooke this yong gallaunt of *Troy*, ftrayned hys fhips, and brought him with the Lady *Helena* and the reft of his retinue to the city *Memphis*, where the King at that tyme made his place of abiding. Beeing arriued at the Court, the King afked *Alexander* in thefe wordes: Yong gentleman, what are you, and from what countrey are you landed heere in *Ægypt*? *Alex- ander*, who was not to feeke of an aunfwere, with a comely grace made aunfwere to the King, def- crying both his countrey and lynage, the place alfo from whence hee was arriued, and to what coaftes he directed his courfe. And where then

(quoth

(quoth the King) had you this goodly gentlewoman, for fhe feemeth to be a woman of no
common bloud: whereat my youth fomewhat
mammering before he coulde caft the plot of his
excufe, was betrayed by his feruaunts, who in
humble manner on their knees, difciphered to the
King the whole difcourfe of his treafon. The vaf-
fals hauing ended their fpeeche, *Protheus* turned
hymfelfe to *Alexander,* and tucked hym vp with
thys rounde tale: my friende (fayde hee) were
it not for the reuerence I owe to ftraungers, with
whome my cuftome is not to deale by rigour, I
woulde furely pipe yee fuch a daunce for the wicked
villanie wherewith thou haft abufed thyne hoaft
in *Greece,* that all vnthankefull wretches fhoulde
take example by thee how to vfe thofe that
fhewe them courtefie in a forraigne lande. Ah
vnkynde wretche as thou arte, is thys the beft
requitall thou makeft the *Grecian* for hys noble
vfage towarde thee: to bereaue hym of his
mate, the moft comfortable companyon of all
hys daies, and not contente therewyth, lyke an
arraunt theefe thou haft defpoyled hys goodes,
the beft and principall treafures of hys houfe.
Thou mayeft bleffe the tyme tenne thoufande
tymes, that the *Ægyptians* yeelde fuche honoure
to ftraungers: and packe thee hence from my
prefence wyth the reft of thy mates, fwearyng
by

by my crowne, that if hencefoorth thou bee
feene within the borders of *Ægypt*, I wyll account thee as myne enemye. As for thy minion
and the goodes thou haft broughte, I fhall referue, tyll fuche tyme as the *Grecian* fhall come
to reclayme them. By thefe meanes (fayd the
prieftes) came *Helena* into *Ægypt*, whereof alfo
Homer hymfelfe feemed not to be ignoraunt, but
of purpofe rather (for that it fell not out fo
fittingly for hys verfe) hee chofe the other, de-
claring notwythftandyng that fome fuch fame as
thys was bruted abroade, whyche appeareth
manifeftly in hys *Illiads*, where making mention
of the voyage of *Alexander*, he affyrmeth, that
by meanes of a contrarye wynde, hee was toffed
by fea, and recouered the lande at the city *Sydon*
in *Phœnicia :* reade the verfes that are framed
by hym in the prayfe of *Diomedes*, in whych
place thefe lynes are founde.

There were the cloakes of gorgeous hue
fo braue and princely dight,
Made by the dames of Sydony,
fold to the feemely wight
Kyng Pryams fonne, that ftale hymfelfe
a wyfe of royall race,
Queene Helene hyghte, retyryng home,
vnto his natyue place

Touching

Touching the fame in his *Odyſſea*
in thefe verfes.

This poyſon quycke and valerous
whych Polydamna gaue
The wyfe of Thonis, Helen brought,
and carefully dyd ſaue.
Great ſtore whereof in droughty ſoyle
of ſcorched Aegypt groe
Some ſoueraigne good, and other ſome
the cauſe of preſent woe.

In like maner to *Telemachus, Menelaus,*
ſpeaketh in this wife.

And when I ſought to leaue the land
of Aegypt, and retyre,
God hyndred, whome I left vnſerued
by vowes and ſacred fyre.

In thefe verfes *Homer* confeffeth that he
knewe of the wandering of *Alexander* into
Ægypt, forfomuch as the countrey of *Syria* is
bounding vpon *Ægypt,* and the people *Phœ-*
nices vnto whome the city *Sydon* is belonging
are refyaunt in *Syria.* As well thefe therefore
as alfo the place it felfe, are no fmall proofe, nay
rather a moft valerous argumente, that the verfes
wherein it is fayde, that *Alexander* conueying
Helen from *Greece* in three dayes fpace, wyth a
profperous

profperous gale, and quyet fea, arryued at *Troy*,
were rather intruded by fome other poet then
inuented by *Homer*, who contrarywyfe in hys
Illiads maketh mention of his errour by fea.

To leaue *Homer*, and come to the affayres of
the *Troianes*, being defirous to vnderftand of
what truth thefe things were which are bruted to
haue beene done by the *Greekes* at *Troy*, I fol-
licited the matter with the prieftes of *Ægypt*,
who tolde me in fuch manner as themfelues
beforetime had beene aduertifed by *Menelaus*.
After the flight of the Lady *Helen*, there affembled, in the caufe of the kings brother *Menelaus*, a puiffant armie of the *Grecians*, who
embarking themfelues into *Teucria*, and incamping in theyr coaftes, fent in ambaffage to the
city *Troy* certayne of theyr chiefe peeres and
nobles, amongft whome, was *Menelaus* brother
to the Kyng. Beeyng entered the city, they
made clayme of the Lady *Helena*, with the
goodes and treafures fhee tooke wyth her, re-
quyring alfo a fufficient fatisfaction to be made
for the iniurie. Wherevnto the *Troianes* aun-
fwered, that they fpente their fpeech in vaine,
to rechallenge eyther women or goodes of them
which they neuer fawe, alleadging, that the
thyngs they challenged were furprifed by the
Ægyptians: neyther was it reafon why they
fhould

(margin) Of the Troiane warre.

fhould beare the faulte of others, and make refti-
tution of that which they neuer had. Howbeit,
the *Greekes* imagining they had fpoken it in
derifion, to fhift off the fiege for the tyme, bent
theyr whole force agaynft the towne, continuing
the fiege and batterie fo long, tyll they had
brought it to vtter ruyne and fubuerfion.

The citie taken, when *Helena* could not be
founde, and the fame aunfwere was rendered the
Græcians as before, they gaue credite at length
to theyr wordes, and fente *Menelaus* into *Ægypt*
to the courte of *Protheus*, whether beeyng come,
and declaryng the caufe of hys arriuall to the
Kyng, he gaue him greate entertaynemente, re-
ftoring vnto him hys Lady with all his treafure,
without any manner of loffe or imbefelment.

Courtefie
rewarded
with
crueltie.

Neuertheleffe, *Menelaus* for all this courtefie
and royall vfage which he had receyued at the
handes of the King, gaue him but a poupe for
his labour, dooyng to the countrey this iniurie
for a farewell. For indeuouring to depart thence,
and wayting a fauourable wynde to fit hys
purpofe, by meanes whereof, he ftayde a long
tyme in *Ægypt:* to knowe the ftate of hys
voyage, what fortune fhould thereafter betide
vnto hym, he tooke two children of the *Ægyptians,* flewe them, and paunched out theyr
bowels, whereby to take view of his future fuc-
ceffe.

ceſſe. Which beyng knowne, and perceyuing
hymſelfe to be mortally hated and purſued of
the inhabitauntes, he ſped hym thence into the
Iſles of *Africa* lying ouer againſt them, from
whence alſo makyng as good haſte as he coulde,
the *Ægyptians* heard no more tydyngs of hym.
Of all theſe things they were partly informed
by the knowledge of hyſtories, beeyng much
more certayne of ſuch thyngs as were done in
theyr countrey. Thus farre the prieſtes of *Ægypt*
proceeding in diſcourſing of *Helena*, whereto I
adde thys ſurmize of myne owne, that if *Helena*
had beene in *Troy*, no doubt for ought that
Alexander could haue ſayde or done, ſhe had
beene deliuered to the *Grœcians.* For who
woulde thynke that Kyng *Pryamus* wyth the
reſidue of that lignage were ſo madde, that to
the ende *Alexander* might enioy the delighte of
hys Lady, would imperill theyr owne lyues and
theyr childrens, with the flouriſhing eſtate of ſo
famous a citie. In whych fond opinion, if in
caſe they had bene at the beginning, yet vndoubtedly they woulde haue recanted at length
when as many valiaunt ſouldyers of the *Troianes,*
and two or three of the Kings owne ſonnes, (if
any credit may be geuen to the poets) were
moſt lamentably ſlaine by the *Grœcians* in fight.
By theſe things I am driuen to coniecture, that
if

The Queene Helena was neuer at Troy.

if *Helena* had beene in their keeping, *Pryamus* to rayſe the ſiege from the walles of hys city, woulde willingly haue wrought meanes to re-ſtore her agayne. Neyther was *Alexander* heyre apparaunt to the crowne, ſo that his father beeyng crooked wyth age, the adminiſtration of the kyngdome ſhoulde reſt in hys gouerne-mente, one there was betweene hym and home, namely hys brother *Hector,* as well in number of yeares hys elder, as in nobleneſſe of mynde hys better, whome it behoued not to ſmooth vp his brother in hys filthy leachery, ſeeing ſuch imminent perill to threaten not onely him-ſelfe, but alſo the whole kyndred and nation of the *Troianes.* But it was the iuſt plague of God inflicted vppon them for their wickedneſſe, that they ſhoulde neyther delyuer *Helena* whome they had not, nor be credyted of the *Grœcians,* to whome they fayned not, to the ende all men might learne, that they whyche ſtryke wyth the ſwoorde, ſhall be beaten with the ſcabberde, being euermore ſeene, that vpon greeuous in-iuries the gods alwayes powre downe greeuous reuengements. Thus much I thought con-uenient to ſpeake of mine owne fancye.

  After the deceaſſe of *Protheus, Rampſinitus* *Rampſinitus.* tooke vppon hym the rule of the countrey, who in memorie of himſelfe, lefte behynde hym cer-

tayne

tayne porches of ftone, planted weftward agaynft
the temple of *Vulcane*, right ouer agaynft the
whych, ftoode two images of fyue and twentye
cubites in length. One of the which ftandyng
northerly, they call fommer, and the other lying
to the weft, they tearme winter, contrary to all
reafon and order. This King in aboundance of
wealth, and plenty of coyne, fo farre excelled
all thofe that came after hym, that none coulde
go beyonde him, no not approch neere vnto hym
in that kynde: wherefore defirous to poffeffe hys
goodes in fafetie, hee builte hym a treafurie or
iewellhoufe of ftone, one of the walles whereof
bounded vpon the outfyde of hys courte. In
framing whereof, the workeman had wrought
thys fubtile conueyance, one ftone in the wall
hee layde in that forte, that a man might eafily
at pleafure plucke it in or out, which notwithftanding ferued fo fittingly to the place, that
nothing coulde be difcerned. When the building was finifhed, the King caufed his treafure to
be brought into it, minding henceforth to be
fecure and to lay afide all feare of misfortune.
In proceffe of time, this cunning artificer lying at
the poynt to dye, called vnto him his two fonnes,
and difclofed vnto them in what manner he had
prouided for theyr good eftate, in leauing a fecret
and moft priuy paffage into the Kings treafurie,

A tale of a
cunning
theefe.

whereby

whereby theyr whole lyfe myght be lead in most happy and blessed condition. In briefe, hee shewed them all that was done by hym, delyuering them the iust measures of the stone, that they mighte not bee deceyued in laying it agayne, whych the two yong youthes well marking, thought from that tyme forwarde to be of the Kings counsayle, if not of hys court, and to become the priuy suruyers of hys iewellhouse.

Theyr father beeing dead, they made no long delay to put in execution theyr determinate purpose, but repayring to the court by night, they found the stone, which with small force remoouing it from the place, they sped themselues wyth plentie of coyne, and so departed. In shorte space after the Kyng entering hys treasurie, and fyndyng the vessels wherein hys money lay to be somewhat decreased, was exceedingly amazed, not knowing whome to accuse, seeyng both hys seales, whyche he had set on the dore, vntouched, and the dore fast locked at hys commyng thyther. Howbeit, repayring sundrie tymes to beholde hys wealth, and euermore perceyuing that it grewe lesse and lesse, deuised with hymselfe to beset the place where hys money lay with certayne greens or snares to entrappe the theefe in. These subtile merchaunts accordyng to theyr former wont approching the spring head where they

they had dronke fo oft before, one of them
wente in, and groaping for the money, was fo
faft intangled in a fnare, that for hys lyfe hee wift
not how to fhifte, but feeyng hymfelfe in thefe
braakes, hee called hys brother, to whome he
difclofed hys euill happe, willing hym in any
wife to cut off hys head, leaft beeyng knowne
who hee was, they both myght bee ferued wyth
the fame fauce. His brother hearing his counfayle to be good, did as he bade hym, and fitly
placing the ftone as hee founde it, departed home,
bearyng wyth hym the head of hys flayne
brother.

The nexte day the Kyng opening hys iewell
houfe, and efpying an headleffe theefe furprifed
in a ginne, was woonderfully aftonied, feeing
euery place fafe, and no way in the world to
come in or out at.

In this quandary, vncertaine what to thynke
of fo ftraunge an euent, he deuifed yet to go
another way to the wood, caufing the body of
the theefe to be hanged out vppon the walles in
open view to all that paffed by, appoynting certayne to attend in that place, with ftraight
charge, that if they hearde any making moane
or lamentation at the fighte thereof, they fhoulde
foorthwyth attache them, and bryng them to the
Kyng.

The

H

The Mother of thefe two Breethren not able
wyth patiente eyes to beholde the wretched
carkaffe of her pitifull fonne, called the other
brother vnto her, aduifing him by fome meanes
or other, to take awaye hys brothers bodye and
burie it, threatening moreouer, that in cafe he neg-
lected to accomplifhe it wyth fpeede, fhee woulde
open all hys thefte and treacherie to the Kyng.
Whome her fonne endeuouring wyth many
woordes to perfuade, and nought auayling (fo
tender was her affection towardes her childe) hee
fet hys wittes abroache to the framing of fome
fubtyle conceyte, to beguyle and inueigle the
Kyngs watchemen. Pannelling certayne Affes
which hee loaded wyth bottells of fweete wyne,
he proceeded forwarde wyth hys carryage, tyll
fuche tyme as hee came agaynfte the place
where the watche laye, where priuily vnftopping
one or two of hys bottles, the wyne flowed out
in greate aboundance, whereat, fayning as
though hee had beene befydes hymfelfe, hee
piteoufly cryed out, tearing hys hayre and
ftampyng as one vtterly ignoraunte whyche to
remedye fyrfte. The keepers feeying the wyne
gufhe out fo faft, ranne haftely wyth pottes and
cannes to receyue it leaft all fhould bee loft, but
the dryuer (who had alreadye caft hys plotte)
feemed heercat muche more inraged then before,

The affection of a mother.

tauntyng

tauntyng and raylyng at them wyth moſt bitter
and reuiling woordes. Contraryly, the watchmen geuing hym very fayre and gentle language,
hee feemed better contented, leadyng aſyde hys
Aſſes out of the way to newe girde them, and
place his carriage in better order. Manye
woordes grewe betweene them whyles he was
addreſſing hys Aſſes to proceede on theyr waye,
till that one of them bolting foorth a merry ieſt,
cauſed hym to laugh hartily, ſo that lyke a good
fellowe, he beſtowed amongſt them a bottle of
wyne. Which courteſie they all tooke in very
good parte, requeſting hym to ſitte wyth them
for companye, and drinke parte of hys owne coſt.
Whereto hee willingly confenting, they dranke
a caroufe, euery man hys cannikin, tyll the wyne
began to runne of the lyes, whyche thys conpeſ-
mate perceyuing, ſet abroach another bottle,
and began to quaffe afreſhe, whyche ſet my
keepers on ſuch a tantarra, that beeyng well
wetted, they ſet more by three drammes of
ſleepe, then ſyxe ounces of witte. When all
was huſhed, and the watchmen faſt aſleepe, hee
tooke the bodye of hys brother, and in mockage,
ſhauing off the hayre of theyr right cheekes, he
returned home, beyng right gladly enterteyned
of hys mother.

The Kyng feeyng hys deuifes no better to proceede

ceede, but for ought he coulde imagine the
theefe ftill beguyled hym, waxed woonderous
wrath: howbeit, determining to leaue nothing
vnattempted, rather then to let fuch a villayne
efcape fcotfree, he built yet another trappe to
catch the foxe in. He had at that time abiding
in hys courte a goodly gentlewoman his onely
daughter, whome he tenderly loued from her
childhood. This Lady he made of his counfayle,
willing her by the duety of a chylde, to abandon
chaftity for the time, making hirfelfe a common
ftalant for all that would come, on condition
they fhoulde fweare to tell her the fubtileft and
the finfulleft prancke that euer they had playcd
in all theyr lyfe tyme, and who fo confelſed the
facts lately atchieued in imbefileing the Kings
treafure, and ftealing away the theefe, him to
lay hold on, and not fuffer to depart.

The gentlewoman obeying her fathers will,
kepte open houfe, hauing greate repayre vnto
her out of all partes of the countrey. Now the
theefe whyche knewe full well to what intente
the Kyng had done thys, defirous to bee at oaft
wyth hys daughter for a nighte, and fearing the
daunger that myghte enfue, beeyng of a verie
pregnaunt and readie witte, deuifed yet another
fhifte wherewythall to delude the Kyng: he
ftrake off the bande of hys brother that was
dead,

dead, and clofely carying it vnder his cloake, he
repayred to the place where the Kings daughter
lay, who demaunding hym the queſtion as ſhe
had done the reſt, receyued of him this aunſwere,
that the finfulleſt acte that euer he committed,
was to cut off his brothers head, beeing inueigled
in a ſnare in the Kings treaſurie, but the fubtileſt
in that he had deceyued a ſort of dronken aſſes,
whome the King had appoynted to watch the
body. The Lady that had liſtned to his tale,
hearing the newes ſhe longed for, ſtretched out
her hand to lay hold on him, who ſubtilly pre-
fenting her with the hande of his brother,
(which beeing darke, ſhe faſt griped in ſtead of
his owne) hee conueyed himfelfe from her and
was no more feene. The King heereof aduertifed, was ſtricken with ſo great admiration as
well of his wit in deuiſing, as his boldneſſe in
aduenturing, that forthwith he cauſed notice to
be geuen throughout all partes of his gouernement, that in caſe the party whiche had done
theſe thinges woulde difclofe hymfelfe, and
ſtande to his mercy, he woulde not only yeeld
him free pardon, but alfo indue and honour him
with ſo princely rewards as were fit for a perſon
of ſuch excellent wiſedome. My yonker yeelding credite to the Kings promiſe, came foorth in
preſence, and defcried himſelfe, with whome

Rampſinitus

Rampfinitus ioyning his daughter in mariage, did him the greateſt honour he could deuiſe, eſteeming him for the wiſeſt man that liued vpon the earth, holding it for certayne, that the *Ægyptians* excelled all others in wiſedome, amongſt whome he iudged none comparable to hym. The ſame King (ſay they) whiles he was yet liuing, trauelled ſo farre vnder the ground, till

Rampfinitus iourney to hell.
he came to the place which the *Grœcians* call the ſeates infernall, where he played at dyce with the goddeſſe *Ceres,* and ſometimes winning ſometimes loſing, he returned againe at length, beeing rewarded by her with a mantle of gold. In the meane ſpace while *Rampſinitus* vndertooke this voyage to hell, the *Ægyptians* kept holyday, prolonging the celebration till ſuch time as he retyred backe againe, which ſolemne obſeruance, ſince our memory hath bene duely celebrated. But whether this be the cauſe of that ſacred feſtiuall, I dare not auowe, howbeit, the prieſtes ſhewed me a certayne cloake, wouen in the ſpace of one daye, wherewith once ayeare they attyre ſome one of theyr petie vicares, blinding moreouer hys eyes wyth a myter. Beeing in thys ſorte attyred, they conduct hym to the hygh way that leadeth to the temple of the goddeſſe *Ceres,* where after they haue placed hym, they leaue hym grabling in that place, and

departe

departe their waye. To whome incontinently
reforte two wolues, conducting the prieft to the
temple aforefayde, whyche is diftaunte from
the city twentie furlongs, where hauing accomplifhed certayne rytes, the wolues leade hym
backe agayne to the fame place. All thefe
thyngs they doubt not to reporte for certayne
true, which we leaue to euery mans lyking
to iudge of them as they deferue. For myne
owne parte I haue thought it meete to make
relation of fuch things as I heard amongft them,
going no farther in many thyngs then hearefay.

    Amiddeft the infernall powers, the *Ægyptians*
affyrme that *Ceres* and *Liber* haue the chiefe
authoritie.

    The fame people were they that firft helde
opinion that the foule of man was immortall, The opinion
pafling from one body into another by a con- of the Ægyp-
tinuall courfe, as euery one tooke hys beginning ing the
and generation of another, and when it had of the foule.
paffed through all bodyes that haue theyr beeyng
eyther in the lande, fea, or aire, then confe-
quentlie to returne into the bodye of man
agayne, whyche courfe it finifhed within the
tearme of three thoufand yeares whych opinion
had many patrones of the *Græcians*, fome auncient and of great authoritie, others of later
dayes, vfurping and chalenging it for theyr owne,
of

of whofe names I am not ignoraunt, albeit I
minde not to recite them.   The *Ægyptians*
likewife mention that to the tyme of *Rampfinitus,*
religion, iuftice, and true order of gouernement
greatly flourifhed among them.

Cheops.

After whome, the royall dignitie came into
the handes of *Cheops,* a man fraught with all
kynde of vicious demeanour, and wicked con-
uerfation.   For caufing the temples of the gods
to be faft locked vp, he gaue out through all
quarters of hys Empyre, that it myght not be
lawfull for any *Ægyptian* to offer facrifice, to
the ende, that beeing feduced from the feruice
and reuerence of the gods, he might fecurely
employ them in hys owne affayres.   Some
were appoynted to digge ftones in the mountayne *Arabicus,* and from thence, to conuey
them to the riuer *Nilus,* where they were receyued of others which pheryed them ouer the
riuer to the roote of a greate hill named *Africus.*
The whole number of thofe that were conuerfaunt in the Kings affayres, was tenne thoufande
men, feruing by turnes, euery three monethes a
thoufand.   In which manner, he helde the people
the fpace of tenne yeares, in all whiche tyme,
they did nothyng but hewe and cary ftones, a
labour of no leffe importaunce (in my iudgemente)
then to haue built the pyre it felfe, or towre

of

of ftone, which is in length fiue furlongs, in
breadth tenne paces, and in height where it
is greateft, to the number of eyght paces, beeyng
framed of ftone, curioufly carued and ingrauen
with the pictures of beaftes.   Heerein alfo were The building
confumed other tenne yeares, caufing certayne Aegyptian
chambers to be cut out vnder the grounde, Pyramides.
vndermining the ftoneworke vp on the which
the towres were founded, whyche hee prouided
for hys fepulcher.   The fituation heere of was
in a fmall Ilande, through the whyche by a
trench or fmall draught, he caufed the riuer to
haue paffage.   The pyre was made flearewife,
afcending by fleppes or degrees orderly placed
one aboue another.

Hauyng in fuche forte finifhed the lower
worke, they deuifed certayne engines or wreftes
to heaue vp ftones from the grounde to the fyrft
ftayre, and from thence to the feconde, and fo
confequently tyll they came to the place where
the ftone fhoulde lye, hauyng vppon each ftayre
a wreaft : or (that whyche is more likely) vfing
one for all, beeyng framed of lyght wood, to
the intente it might the more eafily be remooued.

The groffe worke finifhed, they began to
polifhe and beautifie the towre from the toppe
downewardes, comming laft of all to the neathermoft ftayre, wherein they made a finall ende and
conclufion

conclufion of the beautie and grace of all theyr
workemanfhippe. In thys pyre, were intayled
certayne letters in the *Ægyptian* language, de-
claring the expence the King was at in the time of
his building, for muftardfeed, oynyons, and gar-
like, which (as I remember) the interpreter told
me, did amount to the fumme of a thoufande
fixe hundred talents. If this were fo, how much
thal we deeme to haue bene fpent upon other
things, as vpon tooles, engins, victuals, labouring
garments for the workemen, being tenne yeares
bufied in thefe affayres: I recken not the time
wherein they were held in framing and hewing
of ftones to fet them in a readineffe for the
mayne worke: neyther all the fpace that paffed
ouer in the conueyance and cariage of the ftone
to the place of building, which was no fmall
numbers of dayes, as alfo the time which was
confumed in vndermining the earth, and cutting
out of chambers vnder the grounde, all whyche
things draue the King to fuch a narrow ftraight,
that he was fayne to cloute out his deuifes with
a moft wicked inuention, which was this: Perceiuing his golden mine to draw low that the
diuell might daunce in the bottome of his bagge
and finde neuer a croffe, he made fale of his
daughters honeftie, willing hir to entertayne
tagge and ragge all that would come, in cafe
they

they refufed not to pay for their pleafure, fithence
Venus accepteth not the deuotion of fuch as pray
with empty hands and threadbare purfes. The
Lady willing to obey the heftes of the King her
father, deuifed alfo the meane to prolong the
memorie of herfelfe, and to aduaunce her fame to
the notice of all ages that fhould enfue, wherefore fhe made requeft to fuche as had acceffe vnto
her, to giue her a ftone to the building and erection of a worke which fhe had determined,
wherewith (as the brute goeth) fhe gaue fo many
ftones as ferued to the framing of a whole pyre,
fituate in the middeft of the three former, in full
view and profpect to the greateft pyrame, which
is euery way an acre and an halfe fquare.

Enfuing the raigne of *Cheops*, whofe kingdome continued the fpace of fifty yeares, the
chiefe gouernement was committed to *Cheph-* Chephrene
renes his brother, which followed the fteps of King of
Ægypt.
his predeceffour as well in other things, as alfo
in building of a pyre, howbeit, not fo huge and
great as that which his brother had finifhed
before him, for we tooke the meafure of them
all. Moreouer, fuch vnderworke wrought out
in caues and chambers vnder the grounde as is
to be feene in the pyre of *Cheops*, are wanting
in this, befides the laborious and toilefome worke
which they had to deriue and drawe the riuer

to

to that place, which hath his courfe through the middeft of the former pyre, hemming in the whole Iland wherein it is fituate: within the compaffe whereof, they affirme that *Cheops* him-felfe was buried. By whome in his lifetime, an houfe was framed of one ftone alone, diuerfly coloured, which he had out of the countrey of *Æthiopia*, forty foote lower then the pire it felfe, yet planted and built vpon the felfefame foundation. *Chephrenes* alfo (by the computa-tion of the *Ægyptians*) ruled the countrey fiftie yeares, by which meanes they make account that their miferie continued an hundred and fixe yeares, al which time, the temples of their gods were vnfrequented, abiding ftill from time to time fealed vp and vnopened, wherefore thefe princes the *Ægyptians* will not name for the hatred they beare them, calling their pyres the towres of the fhepeheard *Philitio*, who at that time kept fheepe in thofe places.

Chephrenes dying, yeelded the Kingdome to *Mycerinus,* the fonne of his brother *Cheops,* who efchuing the wicked acts and deteftable practifes of his father, caufed the temples to be fet open, giuing libertie to the people being fo long diftreffed vnder the gouernement of his father and vncle, to follow their owne affayres, and returne to their auncient cuftome of facri-fice

Mycerinus King of Ægypt.

fice, miniftring iuftice aboue all the Kings that
were before him, for which caufe, none of all
the princes that haue borne rule in *Ægypt* is fo
greatly prayfed and renowned, both for other
caufes which were wifely taken vp by him in
iudgement, and chiefly for this, that a certayne
Ægyptian much complayning that the King
had wronged him in deciding his caufe, he commaunded him to value the loffe which he had
fuffered by him, which the partie doing, he gaue
him fo much of his owne goods to make him a
recompence. *Mycerinus* in this wife gouerning
the common weale with great clemency, and
feekyng by vertue to aduance his fame, was
fodeinely daunted by a great misfortune, the
death of his onely daughter, hauing no more
children but her, which was the firft and greateft
hartbreake that befell him in his kingdome. For
which caufe, being ftricken with forrowe aboue
meafure, and defirous to folemnife her funeralles
by the moft royall and princely kinde of buryall
that could be deuifed: he caufed an oxe to be
made of wood, inwardly vauted and hollow
within, which being layde ouer and garnifhed
moft curioufly with gilt, he inclofed therein the
wanne and forlorne corpfe of his beft beloued
daughter. This royall tombe was not interred
and buryed in the grounde, but remayned vnto
our

our age in the city *Sais* in open view, ftanding
in a certayne parlour of the Kings pallace,
adorned and fet foorth for the fame purpofe,
with moft beautifull and coftly furniture. The
cuftome is euermore in the daye time to caft into
the belly of the oxe fweete and precious odoures
of all fortes that may be gotten: and in the
nighte to kindle a lampe, which burneth by the
tombe till the next daye. In a chamber next
adioyning are certayne pictures of women that
were the concubines of *Mycerinus,* if we may
beleeue the talke of thofe that in the fame city
of *Sais* are profeifours in religion, forfomuch as
there are feene ftanding in that place certayne
mighty images made of wood, twentye or there-
aboutes in number, the moft parte of them bare
and naked, but what women they refemble, or
whofe pictures they be, I am not able to alleadge
more then hearefay, notwithftanding, there were
which as touching the gilded oxe, and the other
images framed this tale, that *Mycerinus* being
inamoured of his own daughter, dealt vnlawfully
with her befides the courfe of nature, who for
intollerable greefe hanging her felfe, was in-
tombed in that oxe by her father: the Queene
her mother caufing the hands of all her gentle-
women to be cut off, by whofe meanes fhe had
beene betrayed to ferue her fathers luft, for which
                                              caufe

caufe (fay they) are thefe images portrayed, to
declare the misfortune which they abode in
their lifetime. But this is as true as the man
in the moone, for that a man with halfe an
eye may clearely perceiue, that their hands
fel off for very age, by reafon that the wood
through long continuance of time was fpaked
and perifhed, whiche euen to our memory
were to be feene lying at the feete of thofe
which were portrayed. The oxe wherein the
yong princeffe lay, was fumptuoufly clad, and
arayed all the body wyth a gorgeous mantle of
Phenicia, hys head and necke beeyng fpanged
and layde ouer with braces and plates of golde
of a maruaylous thickeneffe. Betweene hys
hornes was fet a globe or circle of golde, glifter-
ing as the funne. Neyther is the oxe ftanding
and borne vp vppon hys feete, but kneeleth as it
were on hys knees, equall in bigneffe to a great
heighfer. The manner is once a yeare to bring
this image out of the parlour wherein it is
kepte, hauyng firft of all well beaten and cud-
gelled a certayne image of one of theyr Sainctes,
whome in thys cafe wee thynke it not lawfull
for vs to name. The talke goeth, that the Lady
befought the Kyng her father that beeing dead, fhe
myght once a yeare beholde the funne, whereof
fprang the cuftome and maner aforefayde.

It is as good to be a flave in England as a Sainct in Ægypt.

After

After this, there befell vnto him another miſ-
chiefe that ſate as neere hys ſkirtes as the death
of his dilling, infomuch that he was readie to
runne beyonde hymſelfe for ſorrowe. A prophecie aroſe in the city of *Butis*, that the tearme
of ſixe yeares fully exſpired, the Kyng ſhoulde
ende hys lyfe, leauing hys Kyngdome to be ruled
of another. Whereof the Kyng beeing aduer-
tiſed, and greately greeuing at the rigorous and
vniuſt dealing of the gods, ſped a meſſenger to
the place where the ſeate of prophecie was
helde, to expoſtulate with the god, for what
cauſe (ſince hys father and vnckle who had
beene ſo vnmindfull of the gods, ſhutting vp
their temples, and making hauocke of the
people had liued ſo long) he hymſelfe that had
dealte better with them, and cauſed theſe
thynges to bee reſtored agayne, ſhoulde ſo ſoone
be depriued of the benefite of lyfe, to whome
aunſwere was made, that hys dayes were therefore ſhortened becauſe bee tooke a wrong courſe
and dyd not as he ſhould do, beyng appoynted
by the celeſtiall powers, that the countrey of
Ægypt ſhould ſuffer miſerie, and be afflicted
by their princes the ſpace of an hundred and
fifty yeares, which the two former princes well
vnderſtanding, was neuertheleſſe by him neg-
lected and left vnperformed. *Mycerinus* hearing

ing this round reply, and perceiuing that his
thread was almoſt ſpoon, ſet al at reuell, making
great prouiſion of lights and tapers, which at
euentide he cauſed to be lighted, paſſing the
night in exceeding great mirth and princely ban-
quetting, letting ſlip no time wherein he either
wandered not alongſt the riuer, and through the
woods and groues of the countrey, or entertayned
the time in ſome pleaſaunt deuiſes, following all
things that might eyther breede delighte, or
bring pleaſure, which things he did, to the end
he might prooue the prophecie falſe, and con-
uince the god of a lie, making twelue yeares of
ſixe, by ſpending the nightes alſo as he did the
dayes. *Mycerinus* alſo built a pyre, not equall
to that which his father had ſet vp before him,
beeing in meaſure but twentie foote ſquare,
framed quadrangularly, and another lower then
that, of three acres in compaſſe, being built to
the middeſt of the ſtone of *Æthiopia.* There
be of the *Græcian* writers that ſuppoſe thys
towre to haue bene erected by a woman of
notable fame, called *Rhodope*, who miſſe of their
account, not ſeeming to knowe what that *Rho-*
dope was of whome they ſpeake. Beſides, it is
very vnlikely that *Rhodope* would euer haue
enterpriſed a worke of ſo great value, wherein
infinite thouſands of talentes were ſpent before it

came

*Mycerinus
made twelue
yeares of
ſixe.*

*The ſtory of
Rhodope.*

came to perfection. Laftly, it was not in the dayes of this prince that *Rhodope* flourifhed, but vnder the gouernement of *Amafis,* many yeares paffing from the tyme of thofe princes that planted the pyres, to the dayes and age of *Rhodope.* This gallaunt dame was by countrey a *Thracian* borne, the bondmayd of one *Iadmon,* whofe abiding was in the land of *Samos* in the city of the god *Vulcane,* who in the tyme of her bondage, was fellowferuant with *Æfope* the inuenter of fables, to whome this fmooth minion had a monethes mind and more, for which caufe, being giuen out by the oracle at *Delphos,* that it mighte be free for any man to flay *Æfope* that would, and take pennaunce for his foule for his faulte committed, there was none found that would put him to death, but the nephew of *Iadmon* that came by his fonne, who was alfo named *Iadmon :* whereby we may gather that *Æfope* was a flaue and vaffall to *Iadmon.* The death of *Æfope* wounded *Rhodope* with fo great feare, that fhe tooke her flight foorthwith into *Ægypt,* accompanyed by one *Xanthus* a *Samian,* where fhe fet foorth her felfe to the fale of fuch, as rather then *Venus* fhould be fhut out for a Sainct, thought it no idolatrie to worfhip idols. Whiles fhee abode in *Ægypt,* fhe was redeemed and acquit of her feruitude by one *Charaxus,* who

who purchafed her libertie by a great fumme of
money. This *Charaxus* was of the countrey of
Mitilene, fonne of *Scamandronymus,* and brother
to *Sappho* the notable poetreffe. By thefe
meanes came *Rhodope* to be free, and remayned
ftill in *Ægypt,* where fhe wanne fo great credite
and liking of all men, that in fhorte fpace fhe
grewe to maruellous wealth, beeing fuch as
farre in deede furmounted the degree of *Rhodope,*
but yet amounted not to the buylding of a pyre.
By the tenth parte of whych her fubftaunce, it is
eafie for any man to geffe, that the maffe and
fumme of money which fhe had gathered, was
no fuche myracle as it is made to be. For ftudy-
ing to be famous and remembred in *Greece,*
fhe deuifed a worke which had neuer bene
imagined or geuen by any other, which in re-
membrance of her felfe fhe offered in the temple
of *Delphos.* Wherefore of the tenth parte of
her riches which fhe fente to the temple, fhe
commaunded fo many yron fpittes to be made
(which were imployed to the rofting of oxen) as
the quantitie of the money woulde afoorde that
was fente thyther by her. Thefe fpittes at this
prefent ftande behynde the aultare, whiche the
people of *Chios* erected iuft ouer againft the
temple. Howbeit, fuch arrant honeft women
as are fifhe for euery man, haue in no place the

like

like credite, as in the city of *Naucrates.* Forfomuch as this ftalant of whome we fpeake, had
her fame fo bruted in all places, as almoft there
was none in *Greece* that had not hearde of the
fame of *Rhodope.* After whome, there fprang
vp alfo another as good as euer ambled, by name

Archidice.   *Archidice,* whofe vertues were blafed very farre,
but not with like fame and renowne as her predeceffour, with whome, *Charaxus* was fo farre
gone, that retyring home to *Mytelene,* he was
almoft befides himfelfe, as *Sappho* maketh mention, inueyghing in verfe agaynft hys folly. We
haue thus far digreffed to fpeake of *Rhodope,* we
will now returne to the text agayne.

Next after *Mycerinus,* enfued the raigne and
Afychis   dominion of *Afychis,* by whome (as the priefts
King of
Ægypt.   report) was confecrated to *Vulcane,* a princely
gallerie ftandyng to the Eaft, very fayre and
large, wrought with moft curious and exquifite
workemanfhip. For befides that it had on euery
fide emboffed the ftraunge and liuely pictures of
wilde beaftes, it had in a manner all the graces
and fumptuous ornaments that coulde be imagined to the beautifying of a worke. Howbeit,
amiddeft other his famous deedes, this pur-
A ftatute   chafed him the greateft dignitie, that perceyuing
againft
borrowers.   the land to be oppreffed with debt, and many
creditours like to be indamaged by great loffe,
he

he inacted foorthwith, that who fo borrowed
aught vppon credite, fhoulde lay to pledge the
dead body of his father, to be vfed at the difcretion of the creditour, and to be buryed by him
in what manner he woulde, for a pennaunce to
all thofe that tooke any thing of loane : prouid-
ing moreouer, that in cafe he refufed to repay
the debt, he fhould neyther be buryed in the
tombe of his fathers, nor in any other fepulchre,
neyther himfelfe, nor the iffue that fhould de-
fcend and fpring of his body.   This prince defiring to furpaffe all that had bene before him, left
in memorie of himfelfe an excellente pyre built
all of clay, wherein was a ftone fet ingrauen in
thefe wordes : *Compare me not to the reft of the
pyres, which I furmount as farre as Iupiter ex-
celleth the meaner gods, for fearching the bottome
of the riuer with a fcoupe, looke what clay they
brought vp, the fame they employed to the building of me in fuch forme and ligneffe as you may
beholde.*   And this did *Afychis* imagine to aduance the fame of himfelfe to the time to come.

After whome, the fcepter was held by one
Anyfis a blynde man, inhabiting in a city called
after his owne name *Anyfis*.   In time of whofe
raigne, *Sabbacus* King of *Æthyopia* inuaded
Ægypt with a mightie power.   Whereat the
poore blinde King greatly affrighted, crope
priuily

Anyfis the next King. Sabbacus vanquifhed Ægypt, ruling 50 yeares. priuily away, and gayned a priuie couert in the marrifhe places of the countrey, leauyng the gouernement to *Sabbacus* his enemie, whiche ruled the fame 50 yeares, whofe actes are mentioned to haue beene thefe. If any of the *Ægyptians* made a trefpafie, he neuer vfed to do any man to death for his offence, but according to the quantity of his fault, to enioyne him to arrere and make higher by forreine fupply of earth and ftone, some parte of the city wherein he dwelt, for which caufe, the cities became very high and eminent, being much more loftely fituated then before. For firft of all in time of *Sefoftris* fuch earth as was caft out of the trenches (which were made to geue the water a courfe to the cities that were farre off) was employed to the eleuation and aduancing of the lowe townes, and now agayne vnder this *Æthyopian* they had increafe of frefh earth, and grew to be very high The defcription of the temple of Diana. and lofty. Amongft the reft, the noble city of *Bubaftis* feemeth to be very haughty and highly planted, in which city is a temple of excellent memory dedicate to the goddefle *Bubaftis*, called in our fpeach *Diana*, then the which, albeit there be other churches both bigger and more richly furnifhed, yet for the fightly grace and feemelynefle of building, there is none comparable vnto it. Befides, the very entrance and

way

way that leadeth into the city, the reft is in
forme of an Ilande, inclofed round about with
two fundry ftreames of the riuer *Nilus*, which
runne to either fide of the path way, and leauing
as it were a lane or caufey betweene them,
without meeting, take their courfe another way.
Thefe armes of the floud are eache of them an
hundred foote broade, befet on both fides the
banckes with fayre braunched trees, ouerfhadow-
ing the waters with a coole and pleafant fhade.
The gate or entry of the city is in heighth 10
paces, hauing in the front a beautifull image,
6 cubites in meafure. The temple it felfe
fituate in the middeft of the city, is euermore
in fight to thofe that paffe to and fro. For al-
though the city by addition of earth was arrered
and made higher, yet the temple ftanding as it
did in the beginning, and never mooued, is in
maner of a lofty and ftately tower, in open and
cleare viewe to euery part of the city. Round
about the which goeth a wall ingrauen with
figures and protraitures of fundry beafts. The
inner temple is enuironed with an high groue of
trees, fet and planted by the hande and induftrie
of men : in the whiche temple is ftanding an
image. The length of the temple is euery way
a furlong.

From the entrance of the temple Eaftward,
there

there is a fayre large caufey leading to the houfe
of *Mercury,* in length, three furlongs, and foure
acres broade, all of faire ftone, and hemmed in
on each fide with a courfe of goodly tall trees
planted by the hands of men, and thus as touching the defcription of the temple. Likewife
they make mention in what maner they fhifted
their hands of the *Æthiopian* prince, who ad-
monifhed in his fleepe by a vifion, haftned his
flight to depart the countrey. There feemed
vnto him one ftanding by his bedfide, willing
him in any wife to affemble together the priefts
of *Ægypt,* and to cut them all afunder by the
wafte : which the King pondering in his mind,
faid thus, I wel perceiue that the gods would
picke a quarrel agaynft me, that by the doing of
fome villany or other, I might either incur their
hatred, or the difpleafure of men, but fince the
time of my rule in *Ægypt,* which by the oracle
was prefined, is nowe exfpired, I will kindle no
moe coales then I may well quenche, wherewith
departing the countrey, he left the gouernement
to the feed of the *Ægyptians,* and retired himfelfe into his owne lande. For abiding beforetime in *Æthiopia* the oracles which the *Æthiopians* vfe, gaue out to the King, that he fhoulde
beare rule 50 yeares in *Ægypt,* which time
being finifhed, *Sabbacus* fore troubled with the

The de-
parture of
Sabbacus.

ftrange

ſtrange ſight of his dreame, of his own proper
wil departed the liſtes of the countrey. Inſuing
whoſe flight, the blinde King forſaking his neſt
in the fennes, came out, and ſhewed his head
againe, exerciſing gouernement as he had done
before, hauing wonderfully inlarged the Iland
where he lay, with addition of aſhes and freſh
earth. For whoſoeuer of the *Ægyptians* came
vnto him either with grayne or other prouiſion,
his manner was to giue him in charge, that
vnwitting to the *Æthiopian* prince (who then
withheld from him the right of his kingdome)
he ſhould preſent him with a loade or two of
aſhes. This Ile before the time of *Amyrtæus*
was vnknowne to any man, named in the
Ægyptian language *Ello*, being in bignes 10
furlongs. Next after whome, the title royall
was reſigned ouer to a certaine prieſt called Sethon.
Sethon, ſeruing in the temple of the god *Vulcane*, by whom, the ſouldyers of *Aegypt* were
abuſed and had in contempt as men vnfit,
and not ſeruing for his purpoſe. Wherefore
beſide other ſlaunderous tauntes and reuiling
words, wherby he ſought at all times to greeue
them, he bereaued them alſo of ſuch lands and
reuenues as had bene graunted vnto them by
the former Kings: for which cauſe, after that
Senacherib King of the *Arabians* and *Aſſyrians*
had

had inuaded *Aegypt* with a mighty power, they
refufed to yeeld him ayd and affiftance in his
warres.   The prieft driuen to this fudden blanke,
not knowing howe to fhift, withdrewe himfelfe
into a clofe parlour, where complayning himfelfe
before his god, he fhewed what great and imminent perils were like to befall him.   As he was
in this fort powring out his teares and pitiful
complaints before his image, he fell afleepe,
where there feemed to appeare vnto him the
ftraunge forme of his god, willing him to be of
good comfort, and meete his enemies in the
field, not fearing the euent of battayle, forfomuch as he would fend him fufficient aide to
affift and fuccour him.   Maifter parfon taking
hart of grace by this bleffed vifion, tooke with
him fuch of the *Aegyptians* as were willing to
follow him, and incamped in *Pelufia*, on which
fide only *Aegypt* lieth open, and may be inuaded
by forreine power, in whofe caufe, not one of
the fouldiers would mooue a foote to followe
him out of dores, but pedlers, tinkers, and
common gadders that ftrayed here and there
about the countrey.   Being arriued at the place
before named, in the night feafon, there came
into the tents of their aduerfaries an huge multitude of field mice, which gnawed their quiuers,
bit in funder their bowftrings, and the braces off
                                                    their

their fhields, that in the morning being disfur-
nifhed of their armour, they betooke themfelves
to flight, not without the loffe of many fouldiers.
Herehence is it that the picture of the fame
prince grauen of ftone, is feene ftanding in the
temple of *Vulcane* with this title and infcription,
Learne by me to feare God. Thus far went the
Ægyptians and their priefts in defcribing the The reward
continual fucceffion of their kings and gouer- of godlinefs.
nours, alleadging that from the firft king vnto
this prieft of *Vulcane* before mentioned, were
341 generations. Three hundred generations
conteine ten thoufand yeares, forfomuch as to
three progenies of men are affigned an hundred
yeares, fo that the refidue of the progenies which
were 41 are valued at 1340 yeares. Likewife
they affirmed, that in the courfe of ten thoufand
three hundred and forty yeares, there appeared
no god in *Ægypt* vnder the proportion and
fhape of a man, neyther coulde any fuch thing
be mentioned to haue falne out vnder the gouer-
nance of any of their princes, howbeit, within Myracles
the tearme of yeares aforenamed, thefe ftrange chanced in
alterations were marked in the Sunne at foure the Sunne.
fundry times. Two fundry times it was feene
to rife from that place where it is now wont to
fall, and in like maner to fet in thofe regions
from whence it now arifeth, which alfo came to
paffe

paffe two feueral times. Infuing which things, there was no change in the countrey, no alteration in any poynt, neither as touching the effects and courfe of the riuer, nor for any maladies, death, or inconueniences in the lande. In like forte, before *Hecatæus* the writer of monuments (by whome in the city of *Thebes* a rehearfall was made of the whole difcent of his ftocke and kindred, fetching his progeny from the cvi.god) the prieft of *Iupiter* did this, (as alfo to my felfe that made no relation of mine alliance) leading vs into a large chappel or houfe of praier, they fhewed vs both the number of our auncetry according to our own account. Wherin alfo ftood the images of certaine chiefe priefts and Bifhops in fuch forme and maner as euery one had led his life, where, by orderly difcent and iffue they fhewed vs in what maner the fonne had euermore fucceeded his father in the office of priefthode, reciting euery one of their images vntill they came to the laft. Heerein alfo they difliked the fpeach of *Hecatæus* and fought to fetch his progeny from the cvi.god, making him another account of his kinsfolke and allies, fhewing him how abfurd a thing it was, and difagreeing from reafon for a man to deriue his iffue from a god. For which caufe, in reciting the genealogies, they difprooued his account in

this

this wife, relating howe each of thefe images
were in theyr fpeach named *Pyromis* which
name they tooke by difcent, the fonne from the
father by lineall courfe to the number of 345,
whofe pictures were ftanding in the fame oratory.
Thefe *Pyromes* (as they termed them) were
fuch men as had no affinity with the gods,
neither coulde chalenge their progeny of any
one of the chiefe nobles and potentates, being
fuch as the *Grecians* call καλὸς καγαθὸς, that is,
an honeft, fimple, and wel meaning man. Of
which fort were al thofe whofe monuments were
extant in the place very far from being allied
with any of the gods.   Before thefe men, the
gods themfelues were rulers in *Ægypt,* hauing
their dwelling and abode together with men.
Notwithftanding, being many in number, they
gouerned not the countrey all at once, but fome
one of them for a time, or ech in courfe, til at
length the fcepter came to the hands of *Orus*
fonne of *Ofiris* whom the *Græcians* call *Apollo.*
The laft and yongeft of al the gods by the
Grecians account, are *Hercules, Dionifius,* and
Pan.   Albeit *Pan* with the *Ægyptians* is a
grandfire god, one of the moft auncientft among
them, in the number of thofe eight that are the
chief and principal.   *Hercules* is reckned in the
number of the xii meaner faints.   *Dionifius*
among

among thofe that are called the iii fainɛts,
iffued of the xii former. From *Dionifius* (who
is faid to be the fonne of *Cadmus* by *Semele*)
vnto this our age, are 6000 yeares. From *Hercules* fprong of *Alcmena* to this time welny 9000.
From *Pan* fonne of *Mercury*, begotten of the
Lady *Penelope*, vnto thefe daies wherin we liue,
the time is not fo long as from the *Troiane* war,
to wit, 8000 yeres or there aboutes. In all thefe
things we leaue it free to euery ones fancy to
follow what he will, our felues beft liking of the
common opinion which is generally receiued of

The Greekes
tooke theyr
faints from
the Aegyp-
tians.

all men. For if thefe gods beeing renowned
with great fame in *Græce*, had there alfo wafted
the whole courfe of their age (as *Hercules* de-
fcended of *Amphytrio*, *Dionifius* of *Semele*, *Pan*
of *Penelope*) happily fome man would haue fayde
that the *Ægyptians* had worfhipped fome other
gods, whiche beeing of the fame name with
thefe before mentioned, were notwithftanding in
time long before them. Now the *Græcians*
themfelves confeffe, that *Dionifius* being begotten by *Iupiter*, was no fooner borne, but he
cleaued faft to his fathers thigh, and was caryed
away by hym into *Nyffa*, which is a towne in
Æthyopia neere vnto *Ægypt*. Of *Pan* they
make fhorte worke, as ignorant in what parte of
the worlde after his birth hee was broughte vp
and

and nourifhed. Whereby it is eafily conie&ured,
that the names of thefe gods came of later dayes
to the eares of the *Græcians,* and that accordyng
to that notice, they began to frame for eache of
them a cradle in *Greece,* as though they had
beene borne there, planting more upon hearefay,
then certaine truth. Thus farre we have followed the fayings of the *Aegyptians,* from hencefoorth minding to fet downe the confente of
others, wherein they accord with the people of
Aegypt as concerning fuch things as were done in
that countrey, adding thereto fuch matters as our
felues haue bene beholders of, and eyewitneffes.

The laft King (beeing as before was mentioned the prieft of *Vulcane*) leauing the feate
imperiall void by his death, the *Aegyptians*
being now at liberty, and yet vnable to liue
without the aid of gouernement, chofe vnto
themfelues 12 princes, deuiding the whole land
into fo many partes. Thefe 12 ioyning betweene
themfelues mutual kindred and affinity, exercifed
the authority and office of Kings, eftablifhing
mutuall league and couenaunts, that none fhould
incroch or gather vpon another, but holding himfelfe fatisfied with an equall portion, fhould liue
in friendfhip and amity with the reft, which
their league and agreement they fought by fo
much the more diligence and warines to confirme

The twelue
Kings of
Ægypt.

firme and ſtrengthen, for that in the firſt entrance to their kingdomes a prophecie was geuen
out, that who ſo dranke of a braſen mazer in the
temple of *Vulcane*, ſhould be King alone ouer
the whole land. When the ſacred rites and
ceremonies obſerued in ſtriking of league and
making couenant were duly accompliſhed, it
liked them all to leaue ſome common monument or worke behinde them to the continuance
of their memories, which they did, making a
labyrinth or maze ſomewhat aboue the poole

The Laby-
rinth.

called *Mæris* toward the city, much more greater
and famous than the brute goeth. This I beheld with mine eies, being named *The Maze of
the Crocodyles :* for if a man would frame his
conieƈture according to the report which the
Græcians make thereof, meaſuring the walles
and beauty of the work after their account,
certes he ſhal giue but a beggerly iudgement of
ſo ſumptuous and magnificent a building. For
albeit the temple of *Epheſus* be an excellent and
worthy monument, and the church or religious
houſe of *Samos*, yet are they nothing in reſpeƈt
of the pires in *Ægypt*, one of the which may
well ſtand in compariſon with all the renowned
works of *Greece*, and yet euen theſe are far excelled and ſurmounted by the labyrinth. In
this princely monument are 12 moſt fair and
ſumptuous

fumptuous haules, whofe gates open oppofit ech
againft other, 6 ftanding north neere adioing
together, the other 6 fouth, garded about with
the fame walls.

The roomes and lodgings therein conteyned,
are of two forts, fome lower, wrought cellarwife
vnder the ground, other aboue thefe, being together in number three thoufand and fixe hundred. Of fuch roomes as were fituate in the
feconde ftory, our felves had the full fight and
viewe, fpeaking no more therof then we beheld
with our eyes, following in the reft the report of
others, forfomuch as the vnder buildings were
kepte couert from the fight of all that were
trauellers, becaufe in them lay the tombes of
thofe Kings that were the founders of that place,
with the bodies and dead carkaffes of the facred
Crocodyles. Thus of the neathermoft houfe we
fpeake by hearefay, of the lodgings aboue view-
ing with our owne eyes, more ftraunge and
wonderfull miracles then could be wrought by
the helpe of men, for the fundry turnings and
windings leading from one chamber to another,
did wonderfully amaze and aftonifh my wits. The defcrip-
Out of the great haules we go into certaine caues that
parlours, wherehence the way leadeth in other Laberinth.
bedchambers, next vnto which are fituate diuers
fecrete lodgings that open into the fixe great
                                        haules,

K

haules, ftanding on the contrarie parte of the
court, all which are coped ouer aboue with
wrought and carued ftone, incompaffed alfo with
a wall of moft fayre and beautifull ftone, ingrauen with fundrie forts of pictures. Euery
one of the haules are layde with fmooth white
ftone, beautified on each fide with a goodly
courfe of pillers. To one corner of the Laberinth is adioyning a pyre or towre of ftone,
being fortie paces, wherein are the pictures of
many ftraunge beaftes hewne out and carued of
ftone. To this towre is a way vndermined in
the ground. Notwithftanding, for all the wonders that are to be feene and marked in the
Laberinth, the poole called *Mœris*, neere bounding vnto the fame, hath (in our iudgement)
fundry things thereto belonging of farre greater
admiration. The compaffe of this ponde is
three thoufande fixe hundred furlongs, and fixty
Schœnes as they tearme them, conteyning allto-
gether as much fpace as the fea coaft of the
countrey of *Ægypt*. The length of the poole
lyeth North and South, being in deapth where
it is higheft fiftie paces. Now that it hath not
fprong naturally in that place, but rather hath
bene wrought and digged by the trauell of men,
this is an euident proofe, for that welnye in the
middeft of the ponde are planted two mightie

towres

towres of ftone appearing fiftie foote aboue the
water, and beeing as much vnder. On the
toppe of ech towre is a great image wrought
of ftone, fitting in a chaire of maieftie, fo that
the towres conteyne in heigth an hundreth paces.
An hundreth full paces do make a furlong of
fixe acres. A pace conteyneth fixe feete, or
four cubites. A foote is foure times the breadth
of the hande. The water of *Mœris* is not
naturally flowing from any fpring belonging
thereto (the grounde beeyng exceedyngly parched
and drie) but is deriued from the riuer, the
water hauing recourfe into the poole euerie
fixe monethes by ebbing and flowing. The fixe
monethes wherein the water is retyring out of
the ponde, the multitude of fifhe which is there
taken, increafeth the Kings fifke euery day by a
talent of filuer, and at fuche time as it refloweth
agayne, it bringeth aduantage of twentie pounde
a daye. Thys poole, the inhabitants affyrme,
fearcheth through the vames of the earth, and
fheddeth his waters into the Syrts or quicke-
fands of *Africa*, vndermining a fecrete courfe
into the mayne land towarde the countreys of
the Weft, faft by the fide of an huge mountayne
which appeareth ouer the city *Memphis.* Now
forfomuch as I could not difcerne how all the
molde fhould be beftowed that was caft out
of

of the poole at the firfte making thereof, being
defirous to knowe what was become of it, I
queftioned with the inhabitaunts of thofe places
as touching the fame, whofe anfwere was, that
it was employde to the rampeiring of the bankes
of *Nilus*, and much of it throwne downe the
riuer, whofe fpeach obteyned the more credite
wyth me, for that I remembred the like thing
to haue bene done at the city *Ninus*, one of the
chiefe cities of *Affyria*. In this city it fell out
in auncient time, that certayne good fellowes
wanting filuer, determined to vifit the Kings
treafurie, who at that time was *Sardanapalus*
abounding with infinite fummes of treafure,
which for that it lay fafely garded vnder the
earth in houfes vndermined for the purpofe,
thefe yonkers aforefayde beginning at their owne
houfes, made a way vnder grounde, directly
leading to the pallace of the King, voyding all
the mold which they digged, into the riuer
Tigris by night, which floweth faft by the
city, vntill they had brought their enterprife
to paffe. After the fame manner it fell out in
Ægypt, in cafting the lake of *Mæris*, fauing
that the one was digged by night, the other by
day, but in this alfo, the greateft parte of the
voyde earth was caft into *Nilus*, and difperfed by
the ftreame. And in this manner fay the *Ægyp-*
tians,

tians, was the poole of *Mœris* firſte made. Now
when as the 12 Kings of *Ægypt* had praćtiſed
equity euery one within his owne territory, they
drew together at a certaine time to do ſacrifice
in *Vulcans* temple, where (as the maner was)
the laſt day of the feſtiuall, the prieſt miniſtred
wine vnto them in certaine chalices of gold re-
ſerued for the ſame vſe, where happily miſſing
of his number, hauing but xi cups for xii
princes, *Pſammitichus* ſtanding laſt, tooke from
his head a braſen coſtlet, and for want of a cup,
dranke therein. In lyke maner fel it out with
the reſt of the princes, that euery one was there
preſente in his headpeece of braſſe. In thus
doyng, it was deemed that *Pſammitichus* meante
no crafte or legerdemayne, but had a playne and
ſimple meaning. Howbeit, it could not ſinke
with the reſt but that he did it of purpoſe, and
comming in mind of the oracle that was geuen
them, that whoſoeuer dranke of a braſen chalice,
ſhould vſurpe the whole empyre alone : weying
his faćte, and finding that it was committed by
errour, they thought it not meete to put him to
death, but depriuing him of the greateſt parte of
his dominion, baniſhed him into the marriſh
countrey, with eſpeciall threates, that he ſhould
not meddle with any parte of the countrey beſides. Notwithſtanding, *Pſammitichus* hauing
put

put to flight *Sabbacus* the Kyng of the *Æthyo-*
pians, and chafed hym into *Syria*, after this
conqueft was acquit of hys exile, and reftored
agayne by thofe *Ægyptians* which are of the
tribe of *Sais*, wherefore, once agayne vfing
gouernement wyth the reft of hys confederates,
for the olde grudge of the brafen helmet, they
forced him to take the fennes agayne. Recount-
ing therefore with himfelfe the great defpight
they had wrought him, determined eftfoones to
reuenge his caufe vpon thofe that had purfued
him, and fpeeding a meffenger to the oracle of
Latona in the citie of *Butis*, which of all the
feates of fouthfaying is of greateft truth, aunfwere
was giuen him to be of good courage, he fhoulde
haue helpe inough by brafen men that fhoulde
arife from the fea. Which prophecie for the
ftrangeneffe thereof could hardly fincke into his
braines, to make him hope for the helpe of
brafen fouldyers. Not long after, certayne
pyrates of *Ionia* and *Caria* proling alongft the
feacoaftes for their pray, were by conftraynte of
weather driuen vpon the fhores of *Ægypt*, where
going on lande all in armour of braffe, a certayne
Ægyptian ranne to *Pfammitichus* in the fennes,
and for that he had neuer before feene any in
the like array, he tolde him that certayne brafen
men were fproong out of the fea to wafte and
                                        defpoyle

Pfammiti-
chus be-
came prince
alone.

defpoyle the countrey. *Pfammitichus* reknow-
ledging the truth of the prophecie, foorthwith
ioyned himfelfe in amitie with the rouers, in-
ducing them by great and large promifes to
abide with him, which being by him in like
forte obteyned, with this frefh fupply of forreyne
ayde, and the helpe of fuch *Ægyptians* as
fauoured his caufe, he prouided againft the reft
of the princes. Hauing the whole gouernement
alone, he made in the city of *Memphis* certayne
porches facred to the god *Vulcane*, lying vpon the
South winde, and oueragainft the porches a fayre
large haule dedicated to *Apis*, wherein the god
Apis at fuche time as he appeared, was releoued
and nourifhed. This place was befet round with
ftately pillers, and ingrauen with fundrie fimili-
tudes and imboffements of beaftes, foules, and
fifhes. Wherein alfo in place of fome pillers
are planted diuers fayre images of no leffe then
twelue cubites in bigneffe. To thefe forreiners
of *Caria* and *Ionia*, by whome he was holpen in
his warres, *Pfammetichus* gaue certayne manner
places to dwell in, lying on each fide of the
riuer *Nilus* called the *Tentes*, whereof beeing
poffeffed, he performed all fuch promifes befides
that were couenaunted betweene them. Moreouer, he put vnto them certayne yong impes
of the *Ægyptians* to be inftruƈted in the
Greeke

Greeke language, from whome, by difcent
of iffue came thofe which are now interpreters
in *Ægypt*, and vfe the Greeke tongue. A
long time did the people of *Ionia* and *Caria*
inhabite thofe places lying againft the fea,
fomewhat aboue the city of *Bulaftis*, fituate
at the mouth of *Nilus*, which is called *Pelufia-
cum*, from whence, they were afterwardes tranflated by King *Amafis* into the city *Memphis* to
gard him againft the *Ægyptians*. After the
Greekes were thus fetled in *Ægypt*, the people
of *Greece* had traffique thither, by which meanes,
fuch affayres as were atchieued in that countrey
from *Pfammitichus* following, are certaynely
knowne of vs without any errour. Thefe were
the firft that inhabited *Ægypt*, being of a diuers
language from the homelings. In like manner,
from whence they fleeted thither, the reliques of
their fhips wherein they came, the olde poftes
and groundreels of their houfes were fhewed me.
And thefe were the meanes whereby *Pfammitichus* obteyned the dominion of *Ægypt*. As
touching the oracle or feate of prophecie, we
haue made many wordes, and will make more,
as of a thing moft worthy to be mentioned.
This oracle is planted in the temple of the goddeffe *Latona* in a great city named *Butis* ftanding againft the mouth of *Nilus* which is called
Sebenniticum,

Selenniticum, into the which they haue entry
that from the vpper parte of the fea cut againft
the ftreame. In this city alfo are the temples
of *Apollo* and *Diana,* and the great pallace of
Latona, wherein is the place of diuination,
hauing a gallery belonging to it tenne paces
high. Heerein fuche things as might lawfully
be feene, and deferued greateft admiration, of
thofe I meane to make report. In this temple
of *Latona* is a fmall chappell framed of one
ftone, whofe walles beeing of equall heigth,
were in length forty cubites : which femblably
was coped ouer the top with another ftone,
beeing foure cubites in thickeneffe. Wherefore
of all thofe things that were pertayning to the
temple, there was nothing that deferued greater
woonder then this little chappell. Next to this
is an Ilande called *Echemmis* ftanding in the
middeft of a deepe and wide lake a little befides An Iland
the chiefe temple, whiche the *Ægyptians* fup- meth.
pofe to fwimme and to be borne vp of the
waters. Howbeit, I neither fawe it fwimme
nor mooue, maruayling very much (if it were
true) that an Iland fhould be caryed in the
waters. In this Ile is planted the temple of
Apollo, a greate and fumptuous building, lykewyfe three rewes of aultares, and many fayre
palme-trees,

palme-trees, fome very kynde and bearing fruite, other fruitleffe and barren.

The *Ægyptians* alfo render a caufe of the fwimming of this Ilande, faying thus: that at what time *Latona* (which is one of the eyght faints that are of greateft antiquity amongft them) dwelt in the city of *Butis* whereas nowe the oracle is helde: fhe tooke the faueguard of *Apollo* commended vnto her by his mother *Ifis*, and preferued hys lyfe in the fame Ilande, beeyng at that tyme ftedfaft and immoueable, when as *Typhon* made fo diligente fearche in all places to finde out the fonne of *Ofyris*. For heere we muft vnderftande, that thys people imagine *Apollo* and *Diana* to be the children of *Dionifius* and *Ifis*, and that *Latona* was but theyr nourfe and bringer vp, that delyuered them from perill. *Apollo* in the *Ægyptian* tongue is called *Horus*. *Ceres* hath the name of *Ifis*: *Diana*, of *Bubaftis*, from whence *Æfchilus* the fonne of *Euphorion* drew his opinion, which alone of all the reft of the poets maketh *Diana* daughter to *Ceres*, after which euent, the Ile (fay they) became loofe, and was marked to floate and mooue in the water.

Ifis the mother of Apollo.

Pfammitichus gouerned in *Ægypt* 54 yeares, 29 of the which he fpent in the affeige of the great

Pfammiti-chus raigned 54 yeares.

great city of *Syria*, which at length he fubdued.
This city is called *Azotus*, which of all the cities
that euer wee hearde of, fufteyned the longeft
affaulte.

Infuing the raigne of *Pfammitichus*, the
gouernemente of the countrey fell to *Necus* hys Necus King
fonne: by whome, firft of all was the channell of Ægypt.
digged that leadeth to the red fea, whyche afterwardes was caft afrefhe, and made deeper by
Darius the *Perfian.*

The length of thys courfe was foure dayes
fayling, the breadth fuch, as two reafonable
veffels of three oares apeece might well fayle in
it together.

The water which is deriued from *Nilus* into
this channell, floweth into it a little aboue the
city *Bubaftis*, againft a towne of *Arabia* named
Patumon, and fo continueth hys courfe vnto the
red Sea.

They beganne firft to digge from the playne
of *Ægypt* towardes *Arabia*, for all the countrey
aboue the playne is filled and occupyed wyth a
courfe of greate mountaynes neere vnto the city
Memphis, wherein are many pittes and quarries
of ftone, wherefore from the roote of thys mountayne is the channell deriued, continuing a long
courfe towardes the Eaft, vntyll it come to the
place where the hyll parteth in twayne, whyche
diftaunce

diſtaunce and ſeparation betweene the mountaynes openeth to the South regions, and leadeth
to the narrow ſeas of *Arabia.*

In the digging of thys courſe there periſhed
an hundred and twentie thouſande of the people
of *Ægypt.*

When thys enterpriſe was halfe done, *Necus*
brake off and lefte it vnfiniſhed, being diſ-
couraged by a prophecie that tolde hym that
hee toyled for the profite and behoofe of a *Bar-
barian.*

The *Ægyptians* tearme them all *Barbarians*
which are of a ſundry language, *Necus* therefore
leauing hys worke vnfiniſhed, applyed hys ſtudie
to the prouiſion of warre, gathering ſouldyers,
and preparing a fleete of warring Shippes, ſome
of the which were builte at the North Seas,
others in the ſtrayghtes of *Arabia* at the red Sea,
ſome tokens whereof are yet to be ſeene in the
ſame places. Thys Fleete he employed in hys
affayres continuallie ſo long as it fitted hym to
the vſe of warre.

Forſaking afterwards the Sea, and giuing him-
ſelfe to battailes by the land, where, in a conflict
with the *Syrians* at a place named *Magdolos,* he
wanne the renowne of the fielde, and after
the battayle was ended, tooke the greate city
Caditis.

And

The actes
of King
Necus.

And beeyng very neate and fine in hys ap-
parrell, he fent a fute of hys braueſt array to
Apollo in *Branchidæ,* a certayne field of the
Mileſians. In the ende, after he had held the Necus
Kingdome feauenteene yeares, hee then died, raigned 17 yeares.
leauing the title of his foueraignety to *Pſammis* Pſammis
his fonne. During whoſe raigne, a certayne King of the Ægyptians.
people called *Helus* fent meſſengers abrode into
all regions, to giue them to vnderſtand how by
them was deuiſed a game in *Olympus* of greater
admiration and equitie, then by any that euer
had vſed that place, ſuppoſing that the *Ægyptians* (who had the prayſe of wifedome aboue all
nations) could not better or more iuſtly difpoſe
of theſe matters then themſelues. When they
were come into *Ægypt,* and had told the cauſe
of their arriuall thither, the King aſſembled ſuch
of the *Æyyptians* as were moſt excellent for
graue and ſage aduice aboue the reſt. To
whome, when the *Helians* had made difcourſe
of all thoſe things which they had ordeyned in
the fetting foorth of this noble combate, and had
aſked the *Ægyptians* if they could deuiſe any
thing better, after deliberation had of the matter,
they aſked the *Helians* whether they had inacted
that citizens ſhould mayntayne the controuerſie
againſt ſtrangers, or otherwiſe, who aunſwered,
that it was indifferently lawfull for all to ſtriue
of

of what countrey foeuer he were : whereto the
Ægyptians replyed, that it coulde no wife ftande
wyth iuftice, forfomuch as one citizen would
fhew fauour to another, and by that meanes by
partial dealing do iniurie to thofe that came from
farre, fo that in cafe they would order the matter
with more equity, and for that caufe had arriued
in *Ægypt*, it were better to make the game for
ftrangers alone, not fuffering any of the *Helians*
to ftriue.   Thefe things the *Ægyptians* put into
theyr heads and fent them packing.   *Pfammis*
hauing raigned full out fixe yeares, and making
a voyage of warre into *Æthyopia*, incontinently
dyed.

After whome, fucceeded his fonne *Apryes* the
moft fortunateft of all the princes that had ruled
before him, excepting *Pfammitichus* his great
graundfire, gouerning the countrey 25 yeares.
During which time, he warred vpon *Sydon*, and
fought with the people of *Tyrus* by Sea.   Howbeit, fortune owing him a defpight, fhe payde
him home at length, the caufe whereof, we wil
briefely touch at this prefent, deferring a more
ample difcourfe of the fame, till we come to
fpeake of the affayres of the *Punickes*.   When
as therefore vndertaking a iourney againft the
Cyrenians he had fuffered great loffe of his
men : the *Ægyptians* continuing hatred againft
                                                    him,

Pfammis
raigned fixe
yeares.

Apryes King
after the de-
ceaffe of
Pfammis.

him, denied their allegeaunce and rebelled, fuppofing that he had betrayed their liues on purpofe, to the end that with more fecurity he might
gouerne thofe that remained. For which caufe
in great difdayne, afwell fuch as forfooke him
and returned home, as alfo the friends of thefe
that had died in the battell, ftoode at defiance
with the king, renounceing all duties of fubiec-
tion. *Apryes* witting hereof, fent *Amafis* to
treate peace with them : who, when he came
and in many words had rebuked their difloyalty,
one of the *Ægyptians* ftanding behinde him
clapt a Coftlet on his head, faying hee had done
it to make him King. *Amafis* nothing difcon-
tent herewith, was no foner proclaymed King by
the rebells, but forthwith he put himfelfe in a
readineffe to encounter with *Apryes*. *Apryes*
vnderftanding this, fent one of the *Ægyptians*
named *Patarbemes* a man of approued vertue, with
efpeciall charge to bring to him *Amafis* alyue.
Who arryuing fpeedely at the place where hee
was : tolde him the Kinges pleafure. *Amafis*
fittinge on horfe backe and incouraginge thofe
that were about him, commaunded *Patarbemes* to
bring *Apryes* vnto him : *Patarbemes* once agayne
willing him to make fpeede to the King, who
had fente for him : hee anfwered that hee
woulde come with all fpeede poffible, fayinge,
that

Amafis rofe
againft
Apryes.

that the Kinge fhoulde haue no caufe to com-
playne of his flacknelTe, for hee purpofed, god
willing, to bee with him fhortely, and bringe
him more company. *Patarbemes* perceiuinge
by his maner of fpeache and dealinges what hee
was mynded to doe, thought with as much
fpeede as hee coulde to geue notice to the King:
and being returned, *Apryes* in a great rage, for
that hee had lefte *Amafis* behinde him, without
any woordes, by and by commaunded his Nofe
and his Eares to bee cut of. The reft of the
Ægyptians that followed the Kinges partes
feeing this, that fo worthy and renowned a man
fhould without caufe fuffer fo great fhame and
reproche amongft them, without any delay
fled ouer to the rebelles and came to *Amafis*.
Apryes increafing his fury, put in armoure all
fuch as of forrayne countries were hyrelinges in
his hofte (which hee had of *Iönia* and *Caria*,
aboute thirty thowfande men) and marched
agaynft the *Ægyptians*. Hee had in the City
Saïs a very great and gorgeous Pallace. The
armyes therefore of bothe parties, incamped
agaynft other at the City *Memphis*, there to
abide the lot and euent of the battayle.

Nowe the people of *Ægypt* are diuerfly ad-
The trades of men living in Ægypt. dicted, amongft whom are to bee marked feuen
fundry Trades and kindes of liuing: which
are

are thefe : *Priefts, Souldiers, Grafiers, Neate-*
heardes, Salefmen, Interpreters, Maryners : fo
many kindes bee there of this people, taken
of the Trade or crafte which euery one followeth. Likewife, the fouldiers are called
Calafiries and *Hermotylies* dwelling in certayne
regions. For the whole countreye of *Ægypte*
is diftinguifhed into certaine territories. The
coaftes of the *Hermotylies* are thefe. *Bufiris,*
Saïs, Chemmis, Papremis, and the halfe parte of
the Iland *Profopis,* otherwife called *Natho.* In
thefe quarters are inhabyting of the fouldiers
Hermotylies 160 thowfande, none of the which
geue themfelues to manuary artes or any trade
of gayne, but wholly practife the fcience of
armes. Moreouer, to the *Calafyrians* are affigned thefe regions : *Thebana, Bubafliana, Aph-*
thitana, Tanitana, Mendefia, Sebenitana, Athri-
bitana, Pharbæthitana, Thmuitana, Thnuphitana,
Anyfia, Myecphoritana, which tribe poffeffeth
an Iland lying againft the City *Bubaftis.* The
tribes of the *Calafyrians,* when they are muftered
to the moft, yeelde to the warre two hundred
and fiftye thowfand men, which are neuer trained
vp in any thing but in feates of Chiualry the
Sonne learning of his father.

Which cuftome, whether the *Greekes* tooke
from the *Ægyptians,* or borowed it from els
where,

L

Craftsmen of all others leaft in the Land. where, I can not certainely fay, feeing that in *Scythia, Perfia,* and *Lydia,* and welnigh all the countreyes of the *Barbarians,* the bafeft forte of Cityzens are fuch as exercife handicraftes, and their children of leafte accounte: and they beft regarded which are leafte conuerfante in the fame, efpecially fuch as are employed in the fielde.

The fame maner alfo doe the *Grecians* ob-ferue, and chiefly the *Lacedæmonyans,* and euen amonge the *Corinthyans,* craftsmen and fuch others are debafed to the loweft degree.

To thefe gentlemen fouldiers, this chiefe The honour of fouldiers in Ægypt. honour is affigned above all fortes of men, fauing thofe onely that are bufied in the feruice of the Sainétes, that to euery one of them is allotted twelue portions of finguler good grounde, exempt and free from all kinde of Tribute and Penfion, and feuerall to their owne vfe and behoofe. Each plot of grounde contayning euery way an hundred cubyts by the *Ægyptian* meafure. A cubyt amongft the *Ægyptians* is equall to that which they vfe in *Samos.*

A thowfand of each company, afwell of the *Calyfirians* as *Hermatybians,* did yearely geue The Kynges Garde. attendaunce, to garde and defend the Kinges body. To whom, befides the profite and reuen-newes of their land, were certayne Farme-placcs geuen,

geuen, to each man one. Moreouer, for their
lyuery fiue pound of tofted bread, two pounde of
Beefe, and a gallon of wyne, which were duely
ferued to them euery day. When as therefore
Apryes on the one fide with his ftipendaries, and
on the other fide *Amafis* with an huge army of
the *Ægyptians* were come into the City *Memphis*, they clofed battaile : where the hyred
fouldiers of *Apryes* acquited them felues very
valiauntly, till at the length (being fewer in
number) they were put to flight. *Apryes* was
perfwaded that neither god nor the diuell coulde
haue ioynted his nofe of the Empyre, hee feemed
fo furely to haue ftrengthned it to him felfe.
Neuertheleffe, in this fight hee was foyled, taken
a liue, and caried to his owne courte in *Saïs :*
where *Amafis* kept him more like a Prynce than
a pryfoner, for the time that hee lyued. At
length the *Ægyptians* murmuring againfte him,
that hee did not well to referue a liue a mortall
enemy both to himfelfe and the whole country,
he delyuered vp *Apryes* into their handes.
Whom they immediatly toke and ftrangled, The death of
and buried him in the fepulcher of his father in Apryes.
the temple of *Minerua*, neere vnto a certayne
Oratory, at the lefte hand as you enter in. Being
the vfe with the people of *Saïs* to burie all fuch,
as out of their tribe haue attayned to the kingdome,

dome, within the temple. For the toumbe of *Amafis* is placed vppon the other fide of the Oratory, contrary to the Sepulcher of *Apryes* and his Progenitours. Likewife, in one place of this Temple is a fayre Chamber builte of ftone, beautyfied with fundry Pyllers ingrauen like vnto Palme-trees, being otherwyfe very fumptuoufly and royally garnifhed. Iu the middeft of the Chamber are two mayne Pofts, betwene the which ftandeth a Cophine. There is alfo a toumbe in the fame, the name whereof I may not defcry without breache of Religion.

At *Saïs* in the Temple of *Minerua*, beneath the Churche and neere vnto the walle of *Minerua*, in a bafe Chappell, are ftandinge certayne greate brooches of ftone, whereto is adioyninge a lowe place in manner of a Dungeon, couered ouer wyth a ftone curioufly wroughte, the Vaute it felfe being on euery fide carued with moft ex-quifite arte, in biggneffe matchinge with that in *Delos,* which is called *Trochoïdes.* Herein euery one counterfayteth the fhadowes of hys owne affeċtions and phantafies in the nyghte feafon, which the *Ægyptians* call *Myfteryes:* touchinge which, god forbid, I fhould aduenture to dif-couer fo much as they vouchfafed to tell mee. In lyke manner of the Decrees of *Ceres,* which the *Grecians* terme θεσμοφόρια, that is to fay, the

publifhinge

publifhinge of Lawes and Ordynances: of thefe matters I dare not bee very francke in fpeakinge, no further then religion wyll permit. This is certayne, that the Daughters of *Daneus* were the firfte that brought this cuftome oute of *Ægypte,* and made it knowne to the women of *Pelafgos.* But afterwardes miflyked of the *Dores,* it was vtterly abolyfhed and lefte off in all the Countrey of *Peloponnefus,* fauinge of certayne *Arcadians,* whom the people of *Peloponnefus* lycenfed to contynewe in the Countrey, by whome the fame order was retayned.

Apryes being dead *Amafis* raygned in his fteede being of the Tribe of *Saïs,* and trayned vp in a City named *Suph.* In the firft entraunce of his raygne the *Ægyptians* fet lyght by him, and had him in greate contempte, being fpronge of no Noble houfe, but aryfinge of the common troup of the popular forte. Whofe goodwill *Amafis* foughte to reconcile rather by pollicy than feuerity. Being therefore infinitely riche, he had amongeft other his treafure, a Bafen of cleane Golde wherein both him felfe and his Gueftes were wont to wafhe their Feete. This Bafon hee caufed to bee beaten into the forme and Image of a god, and fet it vp in a fit place of the City. The *Ægyptians* repayringe to the place, bowed themfelues in greate reuerence vnto the

The Kinge.

A deuife wrought by Amafis to chafe the goodwill of his fubjeƈts.

the Image : which *Amafis* hauing learned by his friendes, affemblinge the people, tolde them that of the fame Bafen wherein him felfe, and many other of the *Ægyptians* had bene wonte to vomite, pyffe, wafhe their feete, and all fuch bafe exerciles, was framed the god that they fo greatly honoured : faying, that his owne prefent eftate was not much vnlyke vnto that Bafon : for albeit, before time he had bene one of the bafeft degree of the people, yet now being their Kinge hee ought of ryghte to bee had in honour. Whereby the *Ægyptians* weare fo allured that they thought it meete afterwards to obeye their

His cuftome in admini- ftring the kingdome. Prynce.   Who afterwards obferued this Cuf-tome in dealinge with the affayres of the realme : from the morninge, vntill the places of affembly and common meeting were filled, hee fat vppon all matters, that were brought before him : fpend-ing the reft of the day amongft his companyons in fwilling, drinking, and fuch broade and vn-feemely iefting, as if hee had bene fome common rybauld or Vyce of a playe.   Whereat his friendes aggrieuinge, rebuked him in thefe or fuch like termes.   Moft worthy Prince, it is a great ble-mifh to your name to liue fo wickedly, more meete it were for you to fit in a Throne of maiefty and decide the caufes of your fubiects, whereby the *Ægyptians* might knowe them

felues

felues to bee gouerned by a worthy Prince, and
your fame bee increafed throughout all the lande.
To whom hee anfwered. They that owe the
Bowe knowe beft when to bend it : which being
alway bent becommeth fo weake, that it is altogether vnfit for thofe that fhoulde vfe it : euen
fo it fareth with thofe that tyreing themfelues
with continuall paynes, geuing no intermiffion
to their cares, they are fodenly bereaued either
of their right minde, or their perfit members.

This king, whiles hee lyued without honour,
was geuen to bibbing and fcoffing without mea- His nature.
fure, neuer greatly minding his affayres : and as
ofte as hee wanted to ferue his turne, and to
yeelde fupply to his pleafures, he fought mayn-
tenance by filching and ftealing, whereof if
happily hee were at any time attached, his maner
was to ftand ftoutly in deniall of the thing and
defiance of the perfon : for which caufe, being
many times brought to the Oracles and places of
fouthfaying : hee was fometime conuicted by
them, and at other times acquited. Wherefore,
hauing attaynmed to the kingdome, which of the
gods foeuer had acquited him of theft, he had no
regard to their temples, did no honour to them,
gaue no gyftes, offered no facrifice, efteeming
them vnworthy of any reuerence, hauing geuen
out a falfe verdite. And fuch as had pronounced
him

him guilty, to thefe as to the moft true gods, whofe Oracles were agreeable to iuftice, hee perfourmed the greateft honour hee coulde de-uife. Befides, in the City of *Saïs* hee made a porche to the temple of *Minerua*, a worke of great admiration, and farre paffing the reft, both in heights and bigneffe, fo great is the quantity of the ftones that were employed in the building. Hee erected befides in the fame place, diuerfe Images of a wonderfull fize, and the pictures of many noyfome and peftilent Serpents. Hee layde there alfo many huge ftones, to the re-payring of the temple, parte of the which were digged out of the ftone quarryes by *Memphis :* other of great quantity brought from the city of *Elephantina,* which is diftant from *Saïs* 20 dayes fayling. Moreouer, that which is not the leaft wonder, but in my minde to bee reckoned amongft the chiefeft: hee brought from *Elephantina* an houfe framed of one ftone: in the cariage whereof 2000 choyfe men of the Mariners of *Ægypt* confumed three yeares. The roufe hereof on the outfide is 21 cubyts longe, 14 cubits broad, and eight cubites highe: being on the infid 22 cubytes in length, and in height 5. This houfe is fet at the entring into the temple: geuing this reafon why it was not brought into the church, for that the chiefe Mariner,

Mariner, when he had gotten it to that place, as wearie wyth hys dayes worke, tooke refpite and breathed him felfe, whereat the King being very much mooued, bad him leaue of work, not permitting him to labour any longer. Some fay that one of thofe, which were bufied in heauing of the ftone with leauers, to haue bene bruifed to death by it, and that this was the caufe why it ftoode without the Pallace. By the fame King were erected fundry temples, built by arte very exquifitely and cunningly, whereof one hee made facred to *Vulcane :* before which lyeth a great Image with the face vpwarde, in length feuenty fiue feete, being fpread along vppon a pauement of ftone : in the felfe fame place on eache fide this Image, ftand two carued monuments of ftone, twenty foote in quantity. Like vnto this is another ftone in *Saïs,* lying in the felfe fame maner. In like forte the great temple in *Memphis,* fo gorgeous and beautifull to the fight of all that behold it, was the handiwork alfo of the fame King *Amafis.* In the time of this Kinges gouernmente *Ægypt* floryfhed in all wealth, being greatly increafed, afwell by the ryches which the ryuer yeeldeth, as in other reuenewes which the people receyue by the countrey, which at the fame time was fo populous that there were then inhabited 20000 cityes.

Likewife,

Likewife, by this Kinge it was enacted, that
A ftatute of
arrerages. euerye one fhould yearely render accounte to
the cheife prefident of the countrey, howe, and
by what maner of trade hee gayned his lyuinge :
being alwayes prouyding that fuch as refufed to
doe it at all, or bceinge called to a reckoninge,
coulde fhewe no lawefull meanes, howe they
fpent their tymes ; fhould for the fame caufe bee
adiudged to dye.

Which lawe *Solon* borowing of the *Ægyptians*,
did publifh it in *Athens*, and is by them, for the
profite thereof, moft religioufly obferued. *Amafis*
vppon good affection hee bare to the *Grecians*,
befides other benefittes franckly beftowed on
them, made it lawefull, for all fuch as trauayled
into *Ægypte*, to inhabyte the City *Naucrates*.
And fuch as would not abyde in that place,
hauinge more mynde to feafaring for the vfe of
Marchaundize, to thofe hee gaue lybertye to
plant aulters and builde churches. So that the
greateft and moft famous Temple in all the
land is called the *Grecian* temple. The Cityes
of the *Greekes* by whofe charge and expence this
temple was builte in *Ægypte*, were thefe : of the
countrey of *Iönia, Chius, Teus, Phocœa, Clazo-
mene :* amongft the *Dorians* foure Cities: *Rho-
dus, Cnydus, Halicarnaffus, Phafelus :* one City
of the people of *Æolia*, namely, *Mitylene*. To
thefe

thefe Cityes of *Greece* is the Temple belonginge,
by whom alfo are founde and mayntayned certayne Priefts to ferue in the fame. There are
other townes befides in *Greece* that haue fome
righte to the Temple, as hauing contributed fome
thinge to the vfe of the fame.

Howbeit the Temple of *Iupiter,* the people of
Ægina built of their owne proper coft. No
City toke parte with *Samos* in fetting vp the
Pallace of *Iuno :* the *Milefians* alone tooke vppon
them to erect the Temple of *Apollo.* Befides
thefe there are no other monuments built by the
Grecians which remayne extant in *Ægypt.* And
if by fortune any of the *Greekes* pafle into *Nylus,*
by any other way then that which ferueth to
lande from *Greece,* hee is fayne to fweare that
hee was conftrained agaynft his will, byndinge
him felfe by oath that in the fame Shippe he
wyll fpeede him felfe into *Canobicus,* another
Channell of the Ryuer fo called : and if by contrarye wyndes hee bee hindered from arryuinge
there : hee mufte hyre caryage by water, and fo
ferry the nexte way to *Naucrates.* In fuch forte
were the *Grecians* tyed to that City, beinge by
reafon of their trafique thyther, had in principall
honoure. Nowe whereas the Pallace of *Am-
phiction* whiche is nowe at *Delphos,* beeing
ftraungely pearyfhed by fyre, was gone in hande
with

with a frefhe, vppon price of three hundred tal-
lentes : the people of *Delphos* which were
leauyed at the fourth parte of the charges, ftray-
ing aboute all countryes, gathered very much,
being chiefly affyfted by the *Ægyptians.*

Amafis the Kinge, beftowinge on them a
thowfande tallents of Alume, and the *Grecians*
that were abyding in *Ægypt* twenty pound.
Moreouer, with the *Cyrenæans* Prynce *Amafis*
entred friendfhip, and ftrooke a league of fellowfhip with the fame, infomuch, that he thought
meete to enter allyaunce with them, taking a
wife of that countrey, eyther for affection he
bare to the women of *Greece,* or in refpecte of
hys loue to the *Cyrenæans.* His wife, as fome
fay, was the daughter of *Battus* fonne of *Arcefi-
laus,* as others reporte, of *Critobulus* a man of
chiefe credite and regarde amongft thofe with
whome he dwelt. His Ladies name was *Ladyce,*
a woman of furpaffing beautie, with whome, the
King beeing in bed, was fo ftrangely benummed,
and daunted in courage, as if he had bene an
Eunuch, not able to execute any dutie of a man,
wherat the King himfelfe beeing greately agaft,
feeling himfelfe frollicke in the company of other
women, and fo faint to hys Lady *Ladyce,* on a
time began to taunt her in thefe tearmes. Can
it be thou filthy and deteftable hagge, that by
any

any meanes I fhould refrayne from doing thee to the moft miferable death that can be deuifed, which haft thus inchaunted and bewitched my body : In faith minion, I will coniure this diuill of yours, and affure thy felfe, if thy lucke be not the better, thou fhalt not liue two dayes to an ende. The poore Lady ftanding ftiffely in her owne defence, and nothing preuayling to appeafe his fury, vowed within her felfe to the goddeffe *Venus,* that in cafe it might pleafe her to inable *Amafis* to performe the duties of an hufband, and accompany with her the fame night, fhe would dedicate an image vnto her at *Cyrenæ.* Her prayers being heard, *Amafis* became fo frollicke, that before the morning they arofe the beft contented folkes on the earth, euer after that finding hymfelfe fo apt to enioy the delightes of his Lady, that he tooke greateft pleafure in her company, and loued her moft entirely of all other. *Ladyce* remembring her vowe fhe had made to *Venus,* thought good to performe it, and framing a moft beautifull and curious image, fhe fente it to the city *Cyrenæ,* which ftoode vnperifhed vnto our dayes, being placed by the citizens without the towne. The fame *Ladyce, Cambyfes* King of *Perfia* vanquifh-ing *Ægypt* vnderftanding what fhe was, fent her without any manner fhame or violence into her

owne

owne countrey. By this King *Amaſis* were
many giftes diſtributed of ſingulare price and
value. To *Cyrenæ* he ſent the image of *Minerua*,
garniſhed all ouer wyth gilt, and his owne per-
ſonage moſt curiouſly ſhadowed by a Paynter.
Likewiſe to the city *Lindus* he gaue two images
of the goddeſſe *Minerua* wrought in ſtone, with
a linnen ſtomacher moſt excellently imbrodered
by arte. Moreouer, to the goddeſſe *Iuno* in
Samus, two pictures expreſſing her diuine beautie, of moſt exquiſite workemanſhip. Which
bountie he exerciſed towards the *Samians* for
the great friendſhip he bare to their King *Polycrates* the ſonne of *Æaces*. But to the city
Lyndus, why he ſhould ſhewe hymſelfe ſo
franke and liberall, no other reaſon ſerued,
ſauing that the fame wente that the great
temple of *Minerua* in *Lindus* was builded by
the daughters of *Danaus* after they were knowne,
and had eſcaped the daungers intended againſt
them by the ſonnes of *Ægyptus*.
Theſe and many other excellente gifts were diſperſed
and giuen abroade by King *Amaſis*. By whome alſo
the city *Cyprus* which was deemed of all men
inuincible, and had neuer before beene
vanquiſhed by any, was conquer-
ed, taken, and brought
vnder tribute.

_